SINGER TO
THE SEA GOD

SINGER TO THE SEA GOD

VIVIEN ALCOCK

A YEARLING BOOK

Published by
Bantam Doubleday Dell Books for Young Readers
a division of
Bantam Doubleday Dell Publishing Group, Inc.
1540 Broadway
New York, New York 10036

ISBN: 0-440-41003-7

Reprinted by arrangement with Delacorte Press

Printed in the United States of America

March 1995

10 9 8 7 6 5 4 3 2 1

To Nina and Austen

CONTENTS

THESSALIA

AEGAEAN SEA

Sciathos Is.

Peparethos Is.

Scyros Is.

AETOLIA

EUBOEA

Eretria

Chios Is.

ACHAIA

BOEOTIA

ATTICA

Andros Is.

ARGOLIS

Ceos Is.

Tenos Is.

ARCADIA

SARONIC SEA

Syros Is.

Myconos Is.

Farmhouse

Anakharon

Seriphos Is.

Naxos Is.

MESSENIA

Telos

LACONICA

Kapnos Is.

Paros Is.

Siphnos Is.

Melos Is.

Cythera Is.

Thera Is.

CRETAN SEA

0   50   100

MILES

CRETE

MEDITERRANEAN SEA

GDS / Jeffrey L. Ward

I

CLEO

CHAPTER 1

The boy had not been asked to sing that night, the one night he wanted to be there. Now he'd miss the excitement, unless— He thought for a moment. Then he put a clean bandage on his ankle.

Uncle Pelops had sharp eyes. Though the big kitchen was filled with steam from the simmering pots and smoke from the fire and crowded with people, he spotted his nephew as soon as he came in and said, flapping his hands at him: "Go away, Phaidon. You'll only get under our feet, hobbling about like a one-legged duck."

"I'll be careful, I promise. I want to help," the boy said.

"Why aren't you singing for them tonight?"

"Nessus won't let me. He's cross with me because I missed my lesson yesterday. A sprained ankle was no excuse, he said, I didn't sing with my feet or play the lyre with my toes, did I? That's what he said. Please let me stay," Phaidon said, smiling hopefully. "I'll miss all the fun otherwise."

His uncle looked at him, hardening his heart. The boy had an appealing smile; in fact, he was almost as charming as his sister, Cleo. And Uncle Pelops was a kind man, as he was always reminding them. Hadn't he taken them in when their parents had been killed by pirates and their village burned? Hadn't he fed and clothed them when they were small and useless and been both mother and father to them, he, an unmarried man, not used to kids? But there were limits. He was not having the boy in his kitchen, tonight or any other night. There was something about his nephew and the preparation of food that did not go well together. Once let him in, and within minutes food would burn and crockery break, sauces boil dry, eggs roll off tables and smash, and thieving dogs sneak in through doors left open by—guess whom? By his nephew, of course.

There was one now! A thin yellow dog with his paws on the table—

"Get that dog out of here," he shouted, "and go with him!"

"But Uncle—"

"Shoo! Shut the door behind you and don't come back."

"But Uncle—"

"*Go!*" Pelops shouted.

The boy turned as pale as mutton fat, as he always did when anyone shouted. Loud voices frightened him, though he was brave enough in other ways. Sometimes his uncle wondered if he half remembered the raiders coming out of the sea, though he'd been so young then, only just able to walk holding on to his sister's hand. And he'd never spoken of it; neither of them had. Probably it was all for the good. Such things are best forgotten, Uncle Pelops thought, looking at his nephew indulgently. The boy had grown well and had a talent for singing that might well make his fortune one day. He was proud of him, even if the boy was defying him now. He had shoved the dog through the door but remained himself, half in and half out, looking back at his uncle defiantly.

"It's not fair," he complained. "I want to see the mad traveler. I want to see if he's really got a bloody head in his sack, like you said. I've been looking forward to it ever since you told me."

"How was I to know you'd be silly enough to believe it?" his uncle muttered. "The Gorgon's head, indeed! Snakes curling over it instead of hair, or so they say. How do they know what it looks like if he keeps it hidden in a sack, eh?"

"They say it has blood dripping from it."

"They say, they say! They say he's coming so fast that the blood streaks back across the sky like a sunset, and his feet never touch the ground. They'll claim he has wings on his shoes next. People are such idiots." Uncle Pelops threw back his head and laughed loudly, as he always did at other people's folly, being a plain man with both feet on the ground and no clouds in his head.

Nobody else laughed, though he knew they'd all been listening. They might look as if they were concentrating on stirring sauces or chopping herbs, but they weren't. They were waiting to see if he'd give in to his nephew—and they were all on the boy's side.

It's a lonely thing to be a sensible man among fools, he thought, his small eyes filling with self-pity. *Nobody likes you for it. They want to believe in their gods and monsters; they don't thank you for explaining there are no such things in the real world. If I don't let the boy stay, they'll say I'm a fat, greasy bully. I can't help being fat. When you're head cook in the king's kitchen, you have to keep tasting things—how else can you tell if they've been properly done?*

"If you weren't going to let me stay to see the fun, why did you tell me about it?" the boy asked.

"You were there," his uncle said honestly.

Uncle Pelops loved gossip almost as much as he loved food. The market this morning had been humming with the news that Lord

Perseus was on his way back at last, bringing with him in a leather sack his promised gift to the king. Word had come that he'd been seen in Eretria and then on the island of Ceos and would be here in time for dinner, though whether he'd borrow a boat or swim or fly like a bird, nobody could agree. People would believe anything, Uncle Pelops thought, and hurried back, longing to share his amusement with someone. The first person he'd seen was his nephew, Phaidon, sitting in the dusty courtyard, peeling the bark off a stick.

"Why aren't you out with the goats?" he'd asked sharply.

"My ankle," the boy reminded him, pointing to the bandage.

"Oh, yes, of course. Phaidon, you'll never guess what I've just heard," Pelops had said, with a wide smile on his fat face. "Lord Perseus will be here for dinner. We must lay a place for him, eh? And an extra dish for Medusa's head, in case it's still sticky with blood."

"Whose head?" Phaidon asked, interested but ignorant.

"Medusa's. The Gorgon's—oh, you don't know anything! You're too young. You weren't even born when Perseus left," his uncle had said, and had gone off into the kitchen in search of a better audience. But the damage had been done. That's why the boy wanted to help in the kitchen tonight, not because he'd developed a sudden liking for washing greasy dishes but because he wanted to look through the kitchen door into the banqueting hall and see Lord Perseus lay his dripping crimson gift before the king.

"Let him stay, Uncle Pelops," Cleo pleaded. "He can help me. I'll look after him."

Phaidon's sister was a pretty girl, with a cloud of soft black hair and eyes like dark pansies. Her hands were cool and deft and made excellent pastry. It was difficult to refuse her anything.

"Oh, all right," Uncle Pelops said, giving in.

* * *

They went to a table in the corner, out of everyone's way, Cleo rubbing fat lightly into flour with her fingers, and her brother eating raisins out of a blue jar.

"Who is Medusa?" he asked.

"Some sort of monster," his sister said. "They say she had serpents growing out of her head."

"Sounds like a hairdresser's nightmare."

His sister laughed. "Don't you remember the game we used to play? 'The Gorgon will get you!' we'd shout, and all you boys had to shut your eyes and walk on. If anyone cheated and opened his, he'd be stone dead until the end of the game." She rolled her eyes and whispered, "That's what they say Medusa does. One look at her face, and she turns you into stone."

"That's nonsense."

"Perhaps."

"How come Lord Perseus didn't turn into stone if it's true?"

"Perhaps he kept his eyes shut, like in the game."

"How did he know she was there, then?"

"Perhaps she stinks."

"I don't see how he could cut off her head without looking at her," Phaidon said. He put a raisin down on the table, picked up a knife, and, shutting his eyes, tried to cut it in half. He missed. "Why did he promise the head to the king?" he asked.

"I don't know. I wasn't there. I believe the king asked for it. Perhaps he hoped he'd go off and get himself killed. Someone told me they didn't get on. Don't play with that knife, Phaidon. You'll cut your fingers."

Phaidon put down the knife and picked up a spoon. In the back he saw his face reflected, distorted and spoon-shaped, the face of a monster.

"He could've used a mirror!" he cried.

"Who could?"

"Lord Perseus. He could've polished his shield until it shone like a mirror—look, like this plate!" He ran over and picked up a silver plate from a nearby table and held it up so that he could see her laughing face in it. Then he snatched up a wooden spoon and danced up to her, pretending to cut off her head.

"Stop that at once, you stupid boy!" Uncle Pelops shouted, and the assistant cooks, who had been watching and smiling, bent their heads quickly over their work.

A man rode into the front courtyard on a borrowed horse, its hooves clattering on the paving and waking the dozing guard.

"Here! Just a minute!" one of them cried. "Who goes there?"

"Get out of my way."

"But, sir, my lord, you can't—"

"*Get out of my way!*"

The guards were young and did not recognize the traveler. They barred his way with their swords.

"Come, sir, state your name and your business," they said.

"My business? I've brought the king a gift," the stranger told them. "Do you want to see it?" He loosened the drawstring on the heavy leather bag he was carrying and, turning his head away, drew something out. Drops of blood fell from it like petals from a blown rose. "Satisfied?" he asked, and put it back, still without looking at it himself.

The soldiers stood, cold and silent in the moonlight, and could not answer. Pushing past them, the stranger strode into the palace like one who knew his way.

CHAPTER 2

Lord Perseus was late for dinner. The king and his companions had already started. Behind an elaborately latticed screen, the door to the kitchen was fastened back to allow the servants easy access. Young Gordius, coming back for more wine, said breathlessly: "They asked me whom the extra place was for."

"What did you say?" Pelops demanded.

"I said it was for Lord Perseus, and they all laughed at me. They said he was long dead and the crows had eaten him, and even if he wasn't, he wouldn't dare show his face in Seriphos again. But the king was annoyed. I could tell he was. His face went red, and his eyes bulged. He called me a fool."

"So you are, for repeating every stupid rumor you hear," Pelops said, just as if he hadn't been the one to spread it.

"Do you think he'll have me whipped?"

"I wouldn't be surprised. Go and fill your jug and don't keep them waiting, or they may decide to hang you."

"Here, let me fill it for you," Cleo said kindly, seeing the boy was in danger of spilling the wine, his hands were shaking so much. He was a thin, pale boy with lank brown hair and unhappy eyes. She felt sorry for him. "The king won't have you whipped, don't worry. He'll forget about it—and even if he doesn't, he won't remember which one of us you are. We're like cattle to them. They never look at us properly. I bet he calls you 'boy' and doesn't know your name. Just keep out of his way for a time."

"I can't. He's waiting for the wine."

"I'll take it in for you," Phaidon offered eagerly, but Gordius shook his head.

"Thank you, Phaidon, but you'd only upset it all over the king and get us both whipped."

"Let me. I'll do it," Cleo said, her eyes shining with mischief.

"You can't. You're a girl."

"I bet you he never notices. Bet you three sugared plums he never looks at me. I'll show you."

She still had the jug in her hands, and before they could stop her, she whisked through the open door and vanished behind the screen.

"She'll never get away with it!"

"What shall I do? Should I go after her?"

"No. Not unless she's found out. Let's watch," Phaidon whispered.

They stood behind the latticed screen and peered through gaps between the carved foliage. Between two leaves and a wooden apple, Phaidon could see the banqueting hall beyond. It was a large room, lit by ten flaring torches fixed by iron brackets to the stone walls. By their warm and smoky light, he could see the lords and ladies of Seriphos sprawled around the long table, dark figures brightened here and there by the flash of a jeweled ring or brooch and the gleam of a golden chain. At the head the king, a large man with both elbows on the table and a silver goblet in one hand, sat in his gilded chair. His mouth and fingers shone with grease from the roast lamb he'd been eating, and his face was still red, though he did not look angry. He was laughing at something Lord Evander was saying, with his mouth wide open and his yellow teeth showing. Now he banged his goblet on the table and shouted for more wine.

"Boy! Where's that stupid boy!"

Phaidon held his breath as Cleo stepped out of the shadows behind his chair, holding the jug. Her hands were steady as she poured the wine—and she was right, the king did not look at her. Lord Evander did. His thick eyebrows went up, and he gave an appreciative whistle, like a common soldier, and said something to the king. Phaidon could not hear what, for there was too much noise, with the lords talking and laughing, Nessus, the musician, playing unregarded, and the clatter of dishes from the kitchen behind him. He saw the king turn toward Cleo—

Alpha, the king's dog, started barking furiously. A sudden shout went up, and Cleo was forgotten. The king and all his companions were staring at the great doorway opposite, where a solitary man stood, dark as a shadow. He was thin and tall and much travel-stained, his black woolen cloak spattered with mud and ragged at the hem. He carried no sword or spear, but only a large leather bag, badly discolored by streaks of something that shone darkly, wetly in the torchlight. There was something so strangely ominous about him that everyone fell silent. Even the musician dropped his hand from his lyre, leaving a last plucked note to hang vibrating in the smoky air, like the cry of a lost spirit.

"Remember me?" the stranger said at last, his voice loud and harsh in the silence.

"Well, well, if it isn't Lord Perseus," the king said with an easy smile, although Phaidon noticed that his fingers crept toward a sharp knife that lay on the table near his hand. "I hardly knew you. How you've aged. Really, you don't look at all well. You'd better come and sit down—though perhaps you'd like to wash first. You look as though you'd been wading through mud. Tell me, can you still not afford a horse, after all this time, my poor fellow? And what's that you've got in your bag—your dinner? It smells rather high, if you'll forgive my saying so."

The lords laughed.

Before Phaidon could hear any more, a hand grabbed him by the hair and dragged him roughly back into the kitchen. His eyes watered with pain, and squinting up through his tears, he saw it was his uncle Pelops, looking very angry and holding Gordius with his other hand.

"What do you two think you're doing while the rest of us work?" he demanded. "Gordius, we are out of wine. Go and fetch some from the cellar. Quick! On the double!" He pushed Gordius toward the back door and turned to Phaidon. "And as for you—"

"But Uncle Pelops, he's here! I saw him!"

"I don't care what you saw. I want you to— Who let that dog in? What's he got in his mouth? Here, catch him, somebody! Drop it! Bad dog, drop it!"

Gordius had left the back door open behind him, and the thin yellow dog had sneaked in and was now making off with a fat roast goose in its mouth and a fat Uncle Pelops on its heels.

"Better go and help him," one of the cooks advised Phaidon.

"But Lord Perseus has come, and he's got something in his bag, and the king's making fun of him," Phaidon said.

Immediately everyone crowded toward the screen, threatening to overturn it as they pressed against it. Some peered, as he and Gordius had done, through the chinks in the carving. Others, more bold, stood looking around the sides. Phaidon, who was the youngest and therefore the smallest, found himself pushed to the back and unable to see anything at all.

"Let me through," he pleaded, jumping up and down and trying to see over their shoulders. "Please! I can't see! You're too tall." But they took no notice, not even when he thumped on their backs with his fists.

He was going to miss it all. He turned around, looking for something to stand on, and saw on a table an empty silver plate waiting to be filled. He snatched it up, rubbed it hastily on his sleeve, then held it up as high as he could, tilting it in his hand so that he could see over the people in front of him. The screen was too high and he was too far away to be able to see through the small interstices in the carving. He wriggled around to one side and held it up again. Now he could see past the screen and over the intervening heads. Colored shapes swam into his silver plate, distorted by the smoky torchlight and the curve of the metal. The lords were still calling out mockingly and laughing.

Suddenly there was a silence, as if the whole world held its breath. Into the center of his plate came the reflection of a hideous face. Its eyes were cold and dead-looking, its teeth curved over its full but bloodless lips, and around its head small serpents wriggled like maggots on bad meat. Phaidon cried out in terror and dropped the plate with a clatter.

"What was that? Did you see it?" he cried, but the people standing in front of him did not answer. A grayness was creeping over them like old age. Their hair, their necks, even their clothes lost all color. Their warm flesh chilled and hardened into death. When, terrified, he put his hand on a bare arm, it was stone he touched.

"Cleo! Cleo!" he screamed, but there was no answer.

Then one of the stone figures—he could no longer tell who it was—rocked as if the sound of his voice had disturbed its precarious balance and fell heavily to the ground, breaking into three pieces. Sobbing, Phaidon jumped over it and ran into the hall.

The king still sat at the head of the table, but now the red was all gone from his heavy face. His bulging eyes were blind with horror, his mouth gaped open, and his pitted skin was as gray as pumice stone. Never again would he shout at frightened boys and have them whipped.

Beside the gilded chair, Cleo stood quietly, still holding in her hands the silver jug. Her hair, her skin were pale as white marble, delicately veined with gray at wrist and throat. Her clothes were of a darker gray and more porous substance, and the silver jug was blackened where her fingers held it. It was as if whatever malignant force had struck her had, like lightning, passed right through her to alter everything she touched.

All the other faces around the table were contorted with horror, but hers wore only a look of wonder, eyes wide and lips softly parted, as if she had just said "Ah!" Perhaps the monster that had petrified the others, moved to pity by her youth, had turned a kinder look on her.

"Cleo! Cleo!" Phaidon cried, flinging his arms around her and then recoiling in fear. She was as hard and cold as stone.

He heard a noise behind him and, looking around, saw Lord Perseus in his ragged cloak.

"Murderer!" he screamed at him. "Look at my sister! What have you done to her?"

Perseus had slipped his gloved hand into his bag, but now he hesitated, looking from the boy to the marble girl beside him.

"Was she your sister?" he asked. "I'm sorry." He drew his hand out of the bag, empty, and pulled the drawstring tight. "You'd better run away and hide, boy, before the fighting starts," he said, turning away.

"Don't go! You've got to change her back! Take off the spell or whatever it is. Make her well again."

"I can't," the man said, beginning to walk away. "No one can. I'm sorry. Your sister's dead."

Phaidon ran after him and caught him by the arm, but Perseus threw him off roughly, saying, "Don't try me too far, boy. Innocent people suffer in wars. It's always been the way. I can't do anything."

"Who can?" Phaidon shouted after him, and the answer came back, echoing around the room, bouncing from stone figure to stone figure: "No one can. No one can."

Lord Perseus had gone.

CHAPTER 3

Nothing in the room moved except for the flames of the torches and the shadows on the walls. Nobody spoke; nobody shuffled his feet or scratched his head; nobody breathed except for him. Poor Nessus, who had taught him to sing, was dumb now, his fingers frozen on his silent lyre. The king's dog no longer panted but sat with its mouth forever open, and a thread of stone saliva hanging down like a stalactite. Even the flies lay quiet on the table, their stone wings shattered by their fall from the air.

Was he the only person left alive in the world! Phaidon wondered, and pressed his hands over his mouth to stop himself from screaming.

Then Uncle Pelops crept out nervously from behind the screen, followed by Gordius. His uncle's face was gray, but only from fright. The fat cheeks quivered, and he whimpered as he stepped carefully over the broken stone body of his assistant cook.

"Excuse me, excuse me . . . oh, the poor fellow! I can't believe it! I can't!"

"Uncle Pelops! Gordius!" Phaidon cried, running over to them.

"You're all right! Thank the gods, you're all right, dear boy!" his uncle said, hugging him. "And Cleo? Where's Cleo?"

Phaidon could not bring himself to say the word *dead*. "She's like the others," he said, and began to cry again.

"Oh, no! Not my pretty little girl, not Cleo!" Uncle Pelops said, tears running down his fat cheeks. He stretched out his hand as if to pat her but drew it back nervously. "Do you think it's catching?"

"No. How can it be? Lord Perseus brought the Gorgon's head with him— He did! He did!" Phaidon cried, seeing his uncle was shaking his head slowly from side to side. "I saw it. I saw it in the plate—"

"On the plate? Which plate?" his uncle asked, and his eyes swiveled toward the table. *"No, don't look!* We mustn't look or we'll end up like them! Hide your eyes, boys!" he cried, covering his face with his hands.

"Not *on* a plate. Reflected *in* one, like in a mirror. The head's gone now. Lord Perseus took it away in his bag."

"Are you sure?" his uncle asked, lowering his hands cautiously.

"Yes. He said he was sorry. I asked him to change Cleo back, but he said he couldn't. He said the innocent always suffer in war."

"War?"

"He told me to run away and hide before the fighting began. I didn't know what he meant."

"There's often fighting when a king dies," his uncle told him. "Especially when he has no children, no heirs. Well, there's his brother, I suppose, but the king's friends won't want him. . . . Not that this lot are in any state to oppose him." Uncle Pelops looked around at the stone figures with their blind eyes and open mouths. "Don't they look ridiculous? As if they were all waiting to have their teeth pulled." He walked over to the stone king. "Shall I pull your tooth for you, old man? Eh? Or shall I pull your nose?"

"Uncle Pelops!" Phaidon exclaimed, shocked.

"I'm sorry," his uncle said, looking ashamed. "I don't know what came over me. I'm a bit hysterical. He had me whipped once, you know. All because he didn't like the mustard sauce. He got them to hold my mouth open and poured the whole lot down my throat so fast that I choked. I nearly died. Then he had me whipped to teach me a lesson. I have the scars on my back still. Well, I've learned my lesson all right," he added fiercely, turning back to the king. "I'm not dying for you or your brother, old man. Let the rats inherit your throne. Lord Perseus gave you good advice, Phaidon. Let's get our things and be off."

"We must take Cleo. We can't leave her here."

"But, Phaidon, my poor boy, she's not only dead but been turned to stone. We'd never be able to carry her."

"Then I'll stay with her," Phaidon said.

"And I will, too," said Gordius, speaking for the first time since he'd seen Cleo standing there. His face was streaked with tears.

Let him cry, Phaidon thought. *It's all his fault. He should have been the one beside the king's chair, not Cleo. She only took his place because he was frightened.*

Uncle Pelops did not waste time arguing with them. "Very well. Fetch the handcart from the courtyard—and your things. Only be quick about it. We don't know how long we've got. I'll get mine."

The boys ran off, jumping quickly over the assistant cook, trying not to look at their old friends as they passed them. The kitchen was empty. In the courtyard the thin yellow dog, its stomach now bulging with roast goose, was lying in the moonlight. It flipped its tail lazily as they went by.

"I'm sorry. It's all my fault," Gordius muttered. "I should've taken the wine in. She did it for me because I was scared. She's kind; she was always kind. You can kill me, Phaidon. You can kill me if you like. I won't try to protect myself."

"Don't be stupid," Phaidon said. "What good would that do?"

They collected their cloaks. Being slaves, they owned nothing but the clothes they wore and the few oddments they had made for themselves or picked up. Though the handcart wasn't heavy, it was large and bulky. They had difficulty steering it through the kitchen and had to carry it between them over the broken figure of the assistant cook. Gordius had his back to the banqueting hall. It was Phaidon, looking past him, who saw his uncle lift the ornate gold chain over Lord Evander's head and slip it into a bag he'd tied to his belt.

"Uncle Pelops!" he shouted.

"Shh! Don't make so much noise," his uncle said, looking around nervously.

"That's stealing."

"He doesn't need it anymore. What use is it to him?" his uncle muttered. "He can't take it with him."

"They'll hang you for it."

"Who will? Them?" His uncle jerked his thumb scornfully at the stone figures. "You mind your own business, and I'll mind mine, Phaidon. Come on, don't hang about. You and Gordius lift Cleo onto the cart while I finish here."

"Don't take any more!" Phaidon said uneasily.

"Why not? How else are we to live? This is our chance—do you want to be a slave all your life? Free men need goods to trade with, or they're worse off than slaves."

"Robbers are hanged, whether they're slaves or not," Phaidon retorted.

"Shh! Somebody's coming," Gordius said.

Uncle Pelops thrust a gold bracelet hastily into his sack, and they all looked toward the door, listening to the footsteps approach. Two grooms appeared in the doorway and stopped, staring. Behind them the housemaids crept and whispered like mice, their eyes round and bright.

"So it is true," one of the grooms said at last. He was called Dorian, a big man, tall as a young giant. "Lord Perseus did bring the Gorgon's head with him, and this—this cold massacre is the result. What's to do now?" He walked around the table, peering at the stone faces until he found the one he was looking for. "So here you are," he said. "Well, you'll never bawl me out again, my fine lord. Not that you were so bad, I've known worse. It seems I've lost my master—and my living. That won't do. I'll have your belt with its solid gold buckle—oh, and this pretty dagger in its jeweled sheath. And we'll call it quits."

The other slaves came sidling up to the table. Some merely stared in fascination. One woman took a small silver jug, giggled, and slipped it into her pocket. Another removed a shining necklace from a stone lady's neck. A manservant, trying to force a ring over a stone knuckle, lost patience and broke the finger off. Like jackdaws, they fluttered around the table, pecking at the bright trinkets that Uncle Pelops had left. Only one servant wept, an old woman with a face as bleached and seamed as driftwood, who sat at the king's feet, bathing them with her tears.

Phaidon saw his uncle eye the crown on the king's head. It was a pretty thing, made out of gold and silver shaped like leaves. His hand went out but then drew back nervously, almost as if afraid the metal leaves might conceal a hidden serpent.

"Uncle Pelops!" Phaidon called. "Can you help us with Cleo? She's too heavy for us."

Dorian, the large young groom, overhearing this, turned and said: "Not Cleo? Was she caught, poor girl? I thought she'd be safe in the kitchen."

"She should have been," Phaidon said bitterly, and Gordius flushed.

"Let me lift her for you," Dorian offered. He tried to prize the jug out of the marble hands but, finding their hold too tight, put his arms around her and lifted her, jug and all. Strong as he was, he staggered under her weight and would have dropped her had not the boys been quick to help. Red wine spilled out of the silver jug and ran over their hands like blood. Together they lowered her gently into the cart.

"Poor pretty lass," Dorian said, looking down at her. "You were much lighter in my arms when we danced at the spring fair." He took one of the cloaks and laid it gently over her, as if trying to warm her out of her marble sleep. "Where are you taking her?" he asked.

"To some friends on the other side of the island," Uncle Pelops said quickly. "Thanks for your help."

"Are you setting out tonight? You'll need help pushing this cart over the hills."

"We can manage, thank you," Uncle Pelops said. It was obvious to them all that he wanted Dorian to go away. His face was pink, and his expression shifty, and he clinked when he walked.

"As you wish," Dorian said, shrugging. "Let me at least see you on your way."

"No need, no need," Uncle Pelops cried, pushing the cart into the hall and out through the great doors into the courtyard at the front. Seeing the four soldiers of the guard standing with their backs to him, he skidded to a stop.

Dorian walked past him and looked closely at the soldiers. "They won't trouble you, poor creatures," he said. "Lord Perseus must've been this way. See!" He patted a gray soldier on the back, but the man stood unmoving, his drawn sword shining in the moonlight, his stone eyes staring at nothing. "It's quite safe to pass."

He walked to the outer gates with them, then stopped and wished them a safe journey. They thanked him and went out into the road. To the right it ran steeply up the hill before disappearing into the shadow of some low bushes. To the left it ran downhill and disappeared around another corner.

"Did Lord Perseus say where he was going, Phaidon?" Uncle Pelops asked.

"No."

"He'll have gone up to the temple to fetch his mother and Dictys!" Dorian called from the gate.

"Why can't Dorian leave us alone?" Uncle Pelops muttered ungratefully. "He doesn't know any more than we do. I don't trust that young man. He's too big. He must've eaten more than his share of the cake." Raising his voice so that Dorian could hear him, he shouted, "Thank you, thank you! I expect you're right."

"Let's go the other way," Phaidon suggested. "Down to the sea."

"I don't know. Lord Perseus must've come here by boat. Perhaps it waited for him, and he's gone back to fetch his men. We could walk straight into them. Wait a moment." Uncle Pelops knelt down in the road and pressed his ear to the ground. Suddenly he sprang to his feet again, crying out in alarm: "They're coming! I can hear horses! They're coming down the hill. Leave the cart and run for your lives!"

Then he went scampering down the road in the moonlight, without looking back.

CHAPTER 4

Phaidon pushed with all his strength, but as in a nightmare, the cart refused to move downhill. Instead it tilted violently so that Cleo, beneath the cloak that covered her, slid over to one side and nearly overturned it.

"Help me, somebody!" he cried.

Gordius, who had run after Uncle Pelops, stopped and looked around, his eyes and open mouth showing like dark holes in his moonlit face. He hesitated, then began to run back.

But Dorian was there before him, racing out through the gates and into the road. "It's caught on a stone," he told Phaidon, thrusting him out of the way. "Here, let me!"

He pulled the cart toward him, freeing the wheel, and then dragged it off the road and toward some wild olives that had grown together to form a green cave. Gordius joined them, and together they pushed it deep into the leaves until only the tips of the two shafts stuck out like bare branches.

"Keep your heads down," Dorian warned them in a low voice as they crouched down beside the cart, "and your mouths shut."

Phaidon could hear the sound of horses now, and of men shouting, and he began to tremble as the old memories stirred in his head. Peering through the leaves, he saw a band of horsemen come trotting around the corner, their horses' hooves striking sparks off the stony road. Lord Perseus was at their head, his black cloak flying out behind him. Riding beside him was the king's brother, Dictys. They came at their ease, talking and laughing, occasionally shouting some jovial remark to the men behind them. It was obvious they thought they had nothing to fear.

How can he laugh, after what he's done? Phaidon thought, shaking with rage. *And how dare he be sure that nobody is lying in ambush, wanting revenge? Does he think that because we're slaves, we're all cowards?*

Leaning toward Dorian, he whispered, "Lend me your dagger."

The only answer he got was a fierce "shh!"

Before they reached the gate, the riders reined in. Two men dismounted and, drawing their swords, ran quickly into the courtyard. After a moment one of them came out again and beckoned, and the horsemen began to file through the gateway. Phaidon noticed there were six archers among them, holding their short bows at the ready and turning in their saddles to give a last, careful look into the night. So Lord Perseus had taken some precautions after all.

When the last horseman was out of sight, he glanced at Dorian, who shook his head and held his finger to his lips for silence. Phaidon lay still and listened. He could hear nothing but the soft noises of the night, the wind in the leaves, the tiny stirring of small creatures through the grass, a dog barking somewhere.

At last Dorian whispered, "We must keep our voices down. They'll have left a guard."

"I can't see one."

"Nor can I, but they're not fools. Didn't you notice the archers? And every man with a sword by his side. What's to do now? We can't take the cart by the road. Even if they aren't looking our way, they'd hear it rattle over the stones and come running out. The moon's too bright. We'd show up like flies on a white horse."

"The cart's well hidden here," Gordius whispered, "Nobody will find it. It'll be quite safe to leave—"

"No!" Phaidon cried.

"*Shh!*"

There was a short silence while they all listened. No guard came running out of the gate. The road was deserted.

"I'm sorry," Phaidon whispered. "But I can't leave her here as if —as if she's a burden that's too heavy, something to be thrown away. She's my sister. I have to bury her."

The others did not reply. He sensed they were looking at him in the dark, and he did not care if they saw the tears on his cheeks. "She never had anything when she was alive," he said, his voice shaking. "Not since our parents died, nothing she could call her own. Only me and Uncle Pelops. The least I can do is give her a proper burial, with all the necessary rites and hymns and gifts for the gods to see her on her way. If you won't help me move her, I must do it on my own."

"You wouldn't get far without our help," Dorian told him. "There may be some other way. Wait here while I have a look around. And keep quiet."

He slipped out of the shelter of the trees and, bending double so that his fingers nearly brushed the ground, ran like an ape into the nearest shadow and vanished from sight.

"Do you think he'll come back?" Gordius whispered.

"Of course he will."

"He may decide he'd do better on his own."

"Not him. He's brave. He won't run away and leave us."

"I suppose you mean that for me," Gordius whispered resentfully. "I only ran because your uncle told us to and—well, I'm used to obeying his orders in the kitchen. I came back as soon as you called. Didn't I?"

"Shh! Not so loud. Do you want to bring out the guard on us?"

They both turned and looked nervously toward the gateway, but the road was empty in the moonlight, and all they could hear was a dog barking.

"You'd think they'd shut the gates," Gordius whispered.

"Perhaps they've left them open as a trap to catch the king's friends, if he has any left alive. Or his brother's enemies."

The dog yelped shrilly and came racing out of the gates. Two men followed but stopped when they reached the road and contented themselves with throwing stones after it. Then they went back through the gates and out of sight.

"So there are guards," Dorian whispered, returning out of the night as silently as he had gone. "Just as well we didn't risk the road. There's a path of sorts, running down through the scrub toward the sea. It's soft underfoot and should muffle the sound of the wheels, though it'll be rough going. If we're heard, we leave the cart and run. Understood?"

"Yes."

"Right. Gordius, I want you to follow this path until you reach that fir over there, see the one I mean? Go as slowly as you like, but don't make any noise and keep out of sight. When you reach the fir, look around carefully. If the way is clear, wave your arm. If you see anyone, keep hidden until they've gone. Understood?"

"Yes," Gordius whispered, and, crouching low as Dorian had done, moved away. But he was not as silent as the big man had been. Phaidon could hear him stumbling through the bushes and caught occasional glimpses of him as he darted from one shadow to another.

I could have done it better, he thought. *I may be younger, but I'm braver and cleverer, too. Dorian should have chosen me.*

"Why did you want my dagger?" Dorian whispered suddenly.

"I wanted to kill Lord Perseus."

"How?"

"I was going to throw it. I was going to aim for his heart."

"Are you an expert at throwing knives? At so great a distance, a knife you don't know? And by moonlight?"

Phaidon flushed and didn't answer.

"You're a fool," Dorian said, still in that deadly whisper. "Do you know what would've happened? You'd have missed and given away our hiding place. We'd be dead now, the three of us, and what good would that have done?" He paused, as if for an answer, but Phaidon kept silent.

"I very nearly didn't come back," Dorian went on. "I'm young. I don't want to throw my life away on a boy's idiotic dream of revenge. I loved your sister. I was waiting for her to grow up so that I could marry her. You'd have been my brother then. That's the only reason I helped you, for her sake, not for yours. She wouldn't have wanted you to get yourself killed. Forget about revenge. We've enough troubles without looking for more. Forget about it or I'll— Quick! Gordius is waving. Help me with the cart."

It was a hard journey. The ground was uneven. Sharp thistles clawed at their bare legs. Long grasses and low bushes kept entangling the spokes of the wheels. Unseen boulders threatened to overturn the cart, and many times they had to half lift it over ledges of bare rock that stuck out of the shallow earth. By the time they reached the road again, they were exhausted, scratched and bleeding, and glistening with sweat.

The road ran on a little way, then divided, one branch plunging steeply between low cliffs to the beach below. Looking down, they could see dark figures moving on the sands and boats already out on the silvered water, one or two with their sails up and filling with the night wind.

"Can you see Uncle Pelops?" Phaidon asked. "I can't. He must be there somewhere, but . . . where can he have got to?"

"Perhaps he's on one of the boats," Dorian suggested.

"He wouldn't! He wouldn't leave without us!" Phaidon cried, wishing he could be certain that this was true. He heard a dog barking and looked across the bay. A thin yellow dog was dancing and fawning around a man who sat on a rock, his shoulders hunched. It was the dog that had stolen the roast goose and that, obviously recognizing the source, was hoping for more.

The man got to his feet and flapped his hands at the dog, shouting: "Go away! Go away, you greedy creature!"

"Uncle Pelops! Uncle Pelops, we're here!" Phaidon shouted.

His uncle looked around and began running toward them, with the dog bounding beside him, wagging its tail.

They met halfway, on the edge of the sands.

"I thought I'd lost you, dear boy," Uncle Pelops said, hugging Phaidon. "When I looked around, you'd vanished, you and Gordius and— What's *he* doing here? Why does he keep following us?" he added, glaring at Dorian suspiciously.

"We'd never have managed without him. He helped us with the cart," Phaidon told him quickly, afraid Dorian must have overheard what his uncle had said. "We'd have had to leave Cleo behind, but for him."

"Yes, well . . . very kind of him," Uncle Pelops said doubtfully, glancing down at Cleo. Above the cloak, her face shone like a small reflection of the moon above. Her wide-open eyes still held that look of smiling amazement, like a child watching a puppet show. Perhaps that's what she had thought Medusa's head had been, a concoction of paint and linen and wire. "Poor Cleo, poor sweet girl," Uncle Pelops said. "We'll have to—I mean, don't you think that she'd be happier if we left her here on Seriphos, Phaidon? She was born here. This is her home. She won't want to lie among strangers. Besides, she's so heavy. I don't know what the captain would say. She'd hardly count as normal baggage—"

"What captain? What have you done?"

"Don't shout at me, boy! Look around you. Everyone's leaving the island. It's not safe to stay with that maniac about. I don't want to end up like your poor sister. You ought to thank me for hurrying ahead, running all the way till my heart nearly burst. All the little boats are spoken for already. Luckily the trading ship's still in the harbor, and I managed to persuade the captain to take us both, so we'd better hurry."

Both? Just the two of them? Not Cleo, his own niece, not Dorian, who'd risked his life to bring her here, and Gordius, too. Were they to be left behind? Phaidon stared at his uncle disbelievingly, at the fat face glistening in the moonlight, and the cloak bulging out over the bag filled with stolen treasure.

"I'll stay with my friends," he said. "You go on, Uncle Pelops, if you like. Go by yourself. Only remember you can't swim," he added cunningly. "Look at those black clouds over there and the winds coming up. You never know when you might be glad of three strong swimmers like us to save your life."

Pelops looked up at the stormy sky, back at the three of them, then down at the cart where Cleo lay. He sighed heavily and pulled the cloak up over her face, so that she was completely hidden.

"Best not let them see her," he muttered. "People are superstitious, especially seagoing men. They'll say the gods are against us, that she'll bring us bad luck or something stupid like that. Come on if you're coming," he said, looking at them resentfully. "I'll go ahead and fix things with the captain."

With that he scurried off over the sand, grumbling to himself under his breath, and leaving them to follow slowly with the heavy cart.

CHAPTER 5

The trading ship was tied up to a small stone jetty in the harbor, its mast already raised, its oars shipped and sticking up like the quills of a porcupine. Its captain was a Phoenician, a man of middle height, thin and dark. His name was Hiram. He had black hair and a curly black beard, and his eyes were bright and shrewd, a merchant's eyes, used to measuring. He put up no difficulty about taking two extra passengers—as long as it was made worth his while.

"Though I ought to ask for more for the big one since he'll take up so much space," he said, looking with admiration at Dorian, who, helped by Phaidon and Gordius, was half dragging, half lifting the handcart onto the far end of the jetty.

"Ah, but see how small my nephew is," countered Uncle Pelops.

Hiram looked critically at Phaidon. The boy's ankle was hurting badly now, and he was limping heavily. His face was pale and smudged with dirt and tears.

"Is he a cripple?" Hiram asked.

"No, no. He twisted his ankle last week, that's all."

Their voices carried clearly on the wind.

"What does it matter if he's a cripple or not?" Dorian asked, coming up. He set down the cart and stretched his aching arms. "He's not selling the boy to you. Or is he?" He turned fiercely on Uncle Pelops. "Is that your game? Is that why you rushed ahead, so that you could do your bargaining in secret? You'll not sell me!" His hand moved toward his dagger, but then he hesitated, seeing how greatly he was outnumbered, for there were a dozen of the captain's men on the jetty, watching him.

"No, no, you're wrong!" Pelops squealed. "Such an idea never occurred to me—not that I'd have done it, even if it had," he added virtuously. "Quite the contrary. I'm paying for you all. Not only for my ungrateful nephew but for you and Gordius, too. I must be mad. Don't bother to thank me, will you?"

"I don't trade in slaves," Hiram told them mildly. "Not my line. So you can calm down, young man."

Dorian muttered an apology.

The captain nodded. His eyes rested thoughtfully on the jeweled sheath and gold buckle on the belt Dorian was wearing; then he looked at the handcart. "What's in here?" he asked, and before they could stop him, he reached out and pulled back the cloak.

She lay like a lily in the dark cart, her delicate hands still holding the shining silver jug, her blind wide eyes gazing up at the stars in wonder, as if she could hear them singing in the sky. The captain and his men crowded around and looked down at her in silence.

Then the captain said to Uncle Pelops, his voice low and quick: "I'll give you a good price for this. I have a buyer on the mainland, who'd give his eyeteeth for—"

"You said you didn't trade in slaves!" Phaidon cried.

"Slaves? What's the boy talking about? I trade in goods. Are there any more statues like this in—"

"She's not a statue! She's my sister, Cleo."

"Is he mad?" Hiram demanded, and the men muttered uneasily, staring at Phaidon.

"It'd be no wonder, poor boy," Uncle Pelops said. He took the captain by the arm and, leading him a little way off, began whispering in his ear.

"What's he telling him? He doesn't know anything. He wasn't there," Phaidon said, and would have gone to join them, but Dorian pulled him back.

"You keep out of it. You're too rash, you little idiot. You'll get us all into trouble."

"Why, what have I done?" Phaidon demanded indignantly. "And what about you? I saw you go for your dagger."

"It must be catching. Hush now."

Some of the captain's men had been standing nearby, talking in low voices. Now three of them came over and stared curiously down at Cleo. Without thinking, Phaidon pulled the cloak back over her, and they turned their eyes on him, scowling so fiercely that he was frightened. They were wild-looking men with shaggy hair and huge shoulders, their bare arms muscular and their clenched fists showing up like rocks in the moonlight.

"What's the matter?" one of them asked, thrusting his face close to Phaidon's. His teeth were bad, and his breath stank like a sick goat's. "Afraid we're going to steal her, eh?"

Phaidon shook his head.

"Don't try and tell us you came by her honestly," a second one said. "I know runaway slaves when I see 'em. Been robbing your masters, by the look of it. Not that it's any of our business, not unless the captain says so. Tell me, is it true that your king's dead?"

"Yes."

"And all his friends?"

"All who were there."

"What happened?" a third man asked, and now they all came crowding around, their eyes bright and curious in their shadowed faces.

"It was——" Phaidon began, but Dorian interrupted him quickly.

"Some new lord came to dinner, a stranger," he said, choosing his words with care. "At least a stranger to me. He had some quarrel with the king, it seems. There was a fight, and the king was killed."

"The king and all his friends? Must've been some fighter to kill so many single-handed. That is, if he used a sword or spear like any decent man would. But that's not the way we heard it. We heard he brought some foul magic with him." The man lowered his voice and looked fearfully over his shoulder. "Something so monstrous, so frightful——"

"It was the Gorgon's head," Phaidon said before Dorian could stop him.

Immediately the men all began talking at the same time, some claiming it was all nonsense, some swearing it was true and the sooner they were off this accursed island, the better.

"Of course, it's true," a young man with a scarred face shouted. "Why should the boy lie? We all heard him say that the thing in the cart was his sister. Look at it!" He snatched the cloak off Cleo, and they all stared at her. "Do you want to end up like this? Stone, that's what she is, cold stone." He rapped his knuckles on her forehead. Phaidon sprang at him in a fury and was promptly knocked off his feet by a hard fist.

He lay on the ground among a forest of legs and tried to make the spinning world slow down. Confusion roared in his ears like thunder. His head hurt and his ankle hurt and he wanted to sleep, but somebody was prodding him, pulling him, lifting him up. Now he was being carried . . . better than walking . . . but where was he going?

He opened his eyes and saw the mast of the ship only a short way away.

"Cleo? Where's Cleo?" he cried, struggling in Dorian's arms.

"Ye gods, d'you want to have us both in the sea? Save your wriggling till we're safely on board. Cleo's all right," Dorian told him. "Now keep still."

Looking down, Phaidon saw they were crossing a narrow gangplank between the jetty and the ship. He had never been on a big boat before, thirty oars at least and a mast so high it seemed to pierce the moon. The oarsmen were settling down in their places and swore at Dorian as he pushed his way through, still carrying Phaidon in his arms.

"Why don't you throw him overboard as a gift to Poseidon?" one of them suggested sourly, but Dorian only laughed and said he didn't think the sea god would thank them for a mad boy and might send a tempest in revenge.

"Let me down," Phaidon said, struggling, but Dorian only tightened his grip and went on, stepping over legs and ropes and benches, apologizing politely when he was roughly jostled by the men, as if it were his fault, not theirs. Such meek behavior from so large and strong a man frightened Phaidon, and he kept quiet. He could hear the captain shouting something and the slap of ropes against the side of the ship. They were moving now, being thrust away from the jetty by men with stout poles. He saw the thin line of dark water in between widen slowly into a gap too far to jump.

"Here he is," Dorian said, setting Phaidon down on his feet.

Uncle Pelops was sitting huddled up in his cloak, wedged up

against the helmsman's platform in the stern. Gordius stood beside him, looking over the side of the boat.

"Ah, there you are, Phaidon, dear boy," Uncle Pelops said, opening his eyes which had been squeezed shut. "Look after him for me, Dorian, when I'm gone."

"Gone? Where to?" Phaidon asked blankly.

"I think I'm going to die," Uncle Pelops said. He was holding his stomach with both hands, as if afraid it might otherwise decide to jump overboard without him, and his eyes seemed to have shrunk into mere specks in his fat face. "I think I'm going to die," he said again, hoping for tears and sympathy.

"He feels seasick," Gordius explained.

"Seasick?" Phaidon looked over the side. The water in the harbor was as smooth as a silver plate. The prow of the ship was now pointing to the open sea, and suddenly, as a drum began to beat, the oars began to move in perfect unison, down and up, down and up, like the ribbed wings of a featherless bird, scarcely ruffling the moon-bright surface of the sea.

"Sit down over there!" the helmsman shouted. "You, the big one! I can't see through your fat head. And keep the mad boy quiet or he goes into the sea."

Dorian sat down, pulling Phaidon down between him and Gordius.

"Mad boy? Whom does he mean?" Phaidon whispered, and they all looked at him.

"I had to tell them something," Uncle Pelops said in a low voice, looking nervously up at the helmsman, who towered over them on his platform, holding his long steering oar like a weapon. "You shouldn't have mentioned the Gorgon's head. I did warn you. The captain nearly had a mutiny on his hands. The men didn't want us on board, said we were unlucky. I had to tell them you were only a poor mad boy. How was I to know they thought mad boys were unlucky, too? So I said you weren't really mad, but you'd seen your sister killed, so that now you thought you saw her everywhere, in everything—"

"Where is she? What have they done with her?"

"Shh! Don't worry. The captain had her wrapped up in soft fleeces and stored in the hold, while you were still seeing stars," Dorian told him. "He couldn't have taken better care of her if she'd been his own."

"His own? Uncle Pelops, you haven't sold her to him, have you?"

Uncle Pelops groaned and shook his head, holding his hands over his mouth.

The wind was stronger now. They were out of the harbor. The white sail, lowered from its yard, bellied out, and the ship flew over the sea. Thin, dark clouds blew like strands of hair over the pale face of the moon. The oarsmen, their work done for the moment, stirred on their benches and talked of home.

Phaidon and Gordius sat looking over the side. Already the island was fading into darkness, its details vanishing one by one: the beach where they had learned to swim, the trees they had climbed, the rocks they had clambered over, in search of crabs. Soon it would be no more than a black hump against the dark sky.

"I was born on Seriphos," Gordius said.

"So was I."

"Have you ever been anywhere else?"

"No."

"I went to Sisiphos once, that's all."

They were silent for a while, watching their island disappear into the night. Then Gordius leaned over, his lips so near Phaidon's ear that his breath seemed to whistle coldly right through his head.

"They say there are monsters in the sea large enough to swallow a whole ship and all its men," he whispered fearfully.

"That's nonsense."

"Perhaps," Gordius said, just as Cleo had done, when Phaidon had told her the stories about the Gorgon's head were nonsense. And now she was a stone figure, wrapped in sheepskin and lying in the hold of a merchant ship, going the gods knew where.

He crouched on the windy deck, numb with tiredness and grief, his aching head filling with all the travelers' tales he'd heard of a world full of gods and heroes and monsters; of dogs with eyes as big as plates, birds with women's faces, and trees that whispered sad histories into passing ears.

Just before he went to sleep, he opened his eyes briefly and saw two dark figures sitting head to head a little way away, one fat and one with a jutting curly beard, the captain and his uncle. What were they whispering about? Then his heavy eyelids closed again, and he slept.

CHAPTER 6

Phaidon woke from a dreamless sleep into a world of darkness and confusion. All around him, unseen things banged and cracked and groaned. Men were shouting, and high above the din came the wild shrieking of the wind—or possibly his uncle. He could not tell which.

Cold water rushed into his ears and eyes and mouth. It swirled him along, spun him head over heels until he crashed into something both hard and soft, something that swore at him and thrust him away.

Lightning flared in the monstrous sky. He saw he was lying half under a bench on which a huge man sat, groaning as he bent backward and forward over his oar. As the ship tilted once more, Phaidon was thrown against his legs.

"What's that under my feet?"

"It's the mad boy. I said he'd bring us bad luck!"

A hand grabbed Phaidon and dragged him from under the bench.

A scowling face was thrust close to his. He could smell sweat and garlic. Then the man lifted him up into the air, shouting, "He's yours, Poseidon! Take him and spare the rest of us!"

But before he could throw Phaidon over the side, a wave crashed down on them and washed them apart. Phaidon, spinning like a leaf in a torrent, was swept back the way he had come. His outflung hands caught a wooden strut and held on.

"Phaidon! Thank the gods you're safe! Where's Gordius?"

"I don't know. Dorian, it's you, isn't it? Where's my uncle?"

"I've tied him to the rail. That's him muttering and moaning over there. Hold tight! I'm going to look for Gordius," Dorian said, and was gone again.

Phaidon turned his head and called, "Uncle Pelops!"

His uncle did not answer but went on muttering more loudly, as if trying to drown out all other sounds. Phaidon listened in astonishment. Uncle Pelops was *praying*. Praying to the gods he'd always told Phaidon he didn't believe in; he'd always said there were too many gods for a poor man to bother with. "Let the rich make them sacrifices," he'd said. "I can't afford to. They can't expect blood from a bare bone."

Listen to him now: "O gracious Zeus, ruler of the skies, save us! O mighty Poseidon, earthshaker, stirrer of storm and tempest, save us!"

Poseidon. Phaidon remembered the oarsman holding him up and shouting, "He's yours, Poseidon! Take him!" But the sea god hadn't taken him. Instead he'd sent a wave to snatch him out of the oarsman's hands. Had saved his life . . . Why? Why save him and not his poor sister? He didn't care if he joined her. No. That wasn't true. In spite of everything, he didn't want to die.

He wished he knew more about the gods, wished he'd listened when his sister had tried to teach him their names. So many names:

Zeus, Hera, Apollo, Poseidon, Hades, Athena, and—and— The list
went on forever. "Too many to remember," he'd said, yawning. "As
our uncle says, why should we worry about them? They don't worry
about us."

Now he shivered, hearing his uncle cry out: "Save us! Save us!"

Out of the wild night, other voices joined in. "Save us! Save us!"

"You saved me once, Poseidon," Phaidon whispered, clinging to
the rail. "Save me again, and I'll give you—" What could he offer?
He was a slave boy and owned nothing but the clothes he wore, and
they were hardly fit for a god. What else did he have but his bare
skin and his bright eyes and a small talent for singing. "I'll make up
a song for you as soon as I'm safe on land," he promised. The wind
shrieked in his ears.

He did not know how long he crouched there, clinging like a
limpet to the tossing ship, while the tired oarsmen tried to row
them out of the path of the gale.

It was lighter now. He saw to his surprise that they were near
land and that what he had taken for solid night was in fact a high
black cliff rising out of a smoking sea. He cried out in terror, for
they were heading straight for a cleft so narrow that it seemed
impossible for the ship to pass through.

The captain shouted something, and the rowers quickly shipped
their oars, all except three who were too slow. There were three
rapid cracks as their oars broke off as easily as toothpicks; the boat
quivered; then they were gliding quietly between the high cliffs
toward a small, rocky, and inhospitable beach.

Phaidon looked around, dazed by the sudden stillness now they
were out of the wind. He could not see Dorian or Gordius anywhere and felt a sick ache of grief. His uncle, still tied to the rail,
opened frightened eyes and gazed at the tattered sail lying near his
feet and the oarsmen sprawling on their benches.

"Are those men dead?" he asked in a trembling voice.

"Exhausted, I think," Phaidon told him. He tried to untie his uncle from the rail, but the rope was soaked and the knots were tight. He could not loosen them.

"Let me do that," Gordius said, coming up. "I'm good at knots."

"Gordius! You're not drowned!" Phaidon cried, with such obvious relief that the other boy smiled with pleasure. "Have you seen Dorian?"

"He's over there, helping them get the anchors out. We can't get in any closer, because of the rocks, but the water's not deep. As soon as they've made the ship safe, we can go ashore."

"Land," Uncle Pelops said, smiling weakly at the drab gray beach and the forbidding cliffs as if they were a vision of heaven. "Dear land. Where are we, by the way?"

It seemed nobody knew. They'd been blown off course during the storm. They might be anywhere.

They stayed for several days on the stony, uncomfortable beach. When the sun shone straight down into the small cove, they roasted. When it slid down behind the high cliffs, they were cold and miserable. The fire was kept small, for there was little wood to be found, and no fresh water except from the ship's store, and this was carefully rationed. The men, drinking their strong wine undiluted, became drunk and quarrelsome.

The first days they were busy mending the sail, repairing minor damage to the ship, fishing and searching for crabs among the rocks. Their four passengers had offered to help but had been sworn at so fiercely that the captain had stepped between them, as if afraid of trouble.

"I think you'll be more comfortable over there," he'd said, point-ing to the farthest corner of the beach.

"But surely we can help?" Dorian asked.

"Thank you, but there's no need," Hiram told them politely. "This is not the first time we've been caught in a storm. My men know what to do, and you'd only be in their way. If there's anything you want, ask me or Ladon here," he said, indicating the helmsman, who stood at his side. "One of us will bring you your meals. The men are best left to their work. You'll be safe in that corner. Nobody will bother you there."

Though he was smiling, this was unmistakably both an order and a warning.

"They don't want us," Dorian said when they'd settled down in their distant corner. "That's plain enough."

"It's me," Phaidon told him. "They think I'm unlucky."

"I know. I heard them talking. They say the gale was your fault. They have to blame something for it. It makes them feel safer if they think they know the reason for it."

"You mean, get rid of me and there'll be no more gales?"

"Something like that," Dorian said, smiling at him. "So don't wander off by yourself, young Phaidon."

"I won't," Phaidon assured him.

He had wanted to swim out to the ship to see where they had put Cleo but had enough sense not to suggest it. The days seemed endless. Sometimes he and Gordius played games together, bounc-ing flat pebbles over the water or wrestling on the sunbaked rocks. Occasionally they went swimming under the helmsman's watchful eye but were shouted away if they came anywhere near the ship. Sometimes they spent hours trying, unsuccessfully, to catch fish with their hands. At night they took turns to keep watch.

On the seventh day, when Uncle Pelops and Gordius were dozing in the sun and Dorian had gone off by himself to examine some small caves, Phaidon remembered his promise to Poseidon. He went some way off from the others, though still keeping them in sight, and sat down on a flat rock overlooking the water. Though he was a practiced singer, he was not much of a poet. It took him time to find the rhymes he wanted. When at last he was satisfied, he began to sing:

> *In the night of storm we cried on*
> *You to help us, great Poseidon,*
> *Hoping you could be relied on*
> *To save us, save us,*
> *Save us from the hungry fish.*

> *Every want you have supplied on*
> *This sweet island we reside on,*
> *And we thank you, great Poseidon,*
> *Who gave us, gave us*
> *Refuge from the hungry fish.*

He had no sooner finished than he heard a shout of mocking laughter. He flushed and looked around but could see nobody except his uncle and Gordius asleep in the distance, men fishing on the far side of the bay or working on the ship. Besides, it had been a child's laughter, gleeful and jeering.

"Where are you?" he called, confused by the echoes that seemed to come from all around him. There was no answer.

"Where are you?" he shouted more loudly, and, before his own voice had time to echo back at him, heard a muffled giggle coming from the cliff behind him. He turned and stared up at it. A long way up he saw a ledge and a shadow that might have been a cave. But if someone had been there, he was now gone.

"Come back!" he shouted.

He heard footsteps running up and turned to see Dorian, bounding over the rocks toward him.

"I told you not to go off by yourself!" he said angrily. "Who were you shouting at? There's nobody up there. They were behind you. Look!"

"Where?" Phaidon asked, confused. Looking where Dorian was pointing, he saw two of the crew running off toward their side of the beach.

"They crept up on you," Dorian told him, "and hid behind that large rock."

"Oh."

"While you were talking to thin air and laughing like a maniac."

"That wasn't me laughing. It came from up there!"

"What nonsense is this?" Dorian asked wearily. "Haven't we enough trouble without your hearing laughter in the sky. I didn't hear anything. Only you."

"I didn't laugh! I didn't."

Dorian shrugged. "It must've been a bird. You certainly had nothing to laugh about. Those men had stones in their hands."

"You mean—" Phaidon began, his eyes widening. Somehow he'd never really believed that the men would actually hurt him. Most people he knew liked him, even if they occasionally lost their tempers and cuffed his ears. It was one thing to try to throw a boy overboard in the height of a tempest, but quite another to creep up on him, unprovoked, on a sunny day. "You saved my life," he said, looking up at the big man shyly. "Thank you, Dorian."

"They dropped their stones before they noticed me," Dorian told him, smiling. "It was your singing that saved you. As soon as you started, they put down their stones and listened. You have a pretty voice, Phaidon—though I didn't think much of your verse. 'This sweet island,' indeed. This sweet island is likely to be our tomb, unless we can find a way up the cliffs."

"But the ship's been repaired. The captain said only last night that it was ready, and they were just waiting for the wind to change."

"Oh, the ship's ready. It's been ready for two days," Dorian said.

"What is it then? Why do you look like that?"

"I don't know," Dorian said, shrugging and shaking his head. "I'm not a man much given to fancies but . . . it's this island. There's something odd about it. I have a funny feeling—" He broke off and smiled. "Perhaps the wind is changing."

CHAPTER 7

The wind had changed. Uncle Pelops, who had the dawn watch, sat on the uncomfortable stones and watched the stars grow pale and the sky brighten in the east. He yawned. At the mouth of the cove the sea began to glitter and turn gold. He yawned again and thought of food. His eyes closed. His head fell forward onto his chest and he slept.

Four men crept out from behind an outcrop of rock and picked their way carefully toward the sleepers. The two boys had been huddled together, but now Phaidon, perhaps disturbed by the sound of shifting pebble, rolled away from the other boy, flung out an arm, and sighed. But though his eyelids quivered, they did not open.

"You stay here," the man called Creon whispered to his companions. "I'll get him."

He was light on his feet and made no noise. The knife in his hand gleamed in the dawnlight as he crouched over Phaidon. Then he hesitated, not because he was touched by the innocence of the sleeping face but because he was planning how to kill him silently, without waking the others. This must be a stealthy sacrifice, for their captain had forbidden them to harm any of his passengers, even this mad, unlucky boy. "I'm an honest trader, not a murderer," he had said.

And Ladon had backed him up, as he always did, the two men being old friends. The captain alone they might have defied. *Any man can be captain,* Creon had thought. *I could myself. I'm tired of his haughty ways. But a good helmsman is a horse of a different color. Nobody but Ladon can see us safe home again.*

So it must be done quietly. The boy killed, carried away, and thrown into the sea for Poseidon's little fishes, and nobody the wiser. What, had the boy gone? Too bad. Perhaps he had strayed off somewhere and been eaten by a bear. Perhaps he had drowned himself in the sea. Who knows what a mad boy will do?

My left hand over his mouth to stifle his screams, my right sliding the knife up through his ribs into his accursed heart. The point must go in just here, Creon decided, but before either hand had time to move, a flying stone struck him on the back of the head so hard that he fell forward onto the boy, and the knife, missing its target, skidded in a shallow gash over a rib. Phaidon bellowed and wriggled out from under him.

Creon got to his feet and stood swaying, the knife still in his hand. His own blood was running through his hair and down his neck. His friends had fled, and all his enemies were awake now and shouting. But what froze his courage, so that he could not even put up a fight, was the sound of shrill, childish voices ringing out in the empty air above his head, as if the sky were filled with a hundred invisible spirits, all calling out with gleeful malice: "Got you! Got you! You . . . you . . . you!"

He hardly noticed the big man, Dorian, take the knife from his nerveless hand. As in a dream, he allowed himself to be led away over the beach, to where the captain, woken roughly from his sleep by the clamor, was waiting to deal with him.

The ship, sitting quietly on its shadow in the bright water, was crowded with moving figures. The sun had risen clear of the horizon now. The wind was favorable, and soon they would be setting off, leaving behind this stony beach, the grim cliffs, and their four luckless passengers.

"But I paid you," Pelops moaned, hardly able to believe his ears when the captain told him they were to be left in this horrid place. "I paid you well to take us to the mainland. A gold chain and two silver plates! I took you for an honest man."

"I am an honest man," Hiram said stiffly. "Ask anyone along this coast, and they'll tell you so. Here are your two silver plates back—" He touched with his foot a small bag that was lying on the beach with some others. "And here's a sack of grain, some dried fruit, a waterskin, a fishing net, and some rope, all out of our own stores. In exchange, I am only keeping the gold chain and the statue of the girl—"

"No! You can't keep her!" Pelops exclaimed. He glanced quickly across the beach to where his nephew was having his wound seen to by Ladon, who seemed to be a man of many talents. The boy had not heard them. His face was screwed up with the effort of not crying out as Ladon spread some ointment over the shallow gash along his rib. Only Gordius turned and looked at them.

"The boy will be better off without her," the captain said. "Perhaps he will recover from his sickness when the statue is no longer there to remind him of his sister."

There was some truth in that, Pelops thought. He had loved his pretty niece, but the poor girl was dead now. No healer or priest had a magic strong enough to bring her back to life. What was the point of burdening themselves with her heavy marble corpse? Let her find a home in some rich lord's palace, in a cool courtyard, with soft music playing. He almost envied her.

"If I decided to let her go," he said, adding hastily as he caught Dorian's eye, "not that I would, of course, but just supposing . . . I'd expect more for her than these few things. What's a sack of grain compared with a valuable work of art like her, made of the very best materials?"

"The difference between life and death," Hiram pointed out dryly. "You can't eat marble when you're hungry. The price of grain goes up when there's a shortage, anyone knows that. I should take it, if I were you."

"Have we any choice?" Dorian asked.

"No," Hiram admitted.

"And you say you're an honest man!" Pelops cried bitterly.

"*I* am honest," Hiram said, shrugging, "but unfortunately my crew are not. They'd cut your throats with pleasure if I let them. By the way, what happened earlier? Creon's admitted he was out to kill the boy, and he doesn't usually miss his targets—especially when they are asleep. He claims he was hit on the head and has some wild tale of voices in the sky shrieking at him. I suppose the blow he received mixed up his brains."

Dorian shook his head and said that he had heard the voices, too. "Or perhaps only one voice echoing . . . It seemed to come from above, but though I looked everywhere, I couldn't see anyone. Except your man with a knife in his hand and three of your men running away."

"Creon's been whipped," the captain said shortly. "He would not tell me the names of the men with him, but I did not blame him for that."

"This island is haunted," Uncle Pelops whispered, shivering. "There's something here. . . . Take us with you; you must take us with you! Don't leave us in this terrible place. How can I climb those cliffs, a man of my age? I'll hide the boy under my cloak; I'll gag him so he can't speak. Don't leave us here to die. Take us with you!"

"I couldn't answer for your lives," Hiram said. "I'm only one against many. You'll stand a better chance here."

There was a short silence. Then Pelops said sourly, "You'd better go before my nephew finds you're robbing him of his sister. For she *is* his sister. Everything he said is true: Lord Perseus, the Gorgon's head, all of it. He's no more mad than I am. The gold chain you're keeping came off a stone king's neck."

The captain, who'd been staring at him with a mixture of fear and disbelief, bowed stiffly, then turned and walked away, calling for Ladon to come with him. The two boys, left alone, looked after them for a moment, then came running to where Pelops and Dorian stood.

"Are we going now?" Phaidon asked breathlessly. "Ladon's seen to my wound. He said I was brave because I didn't make a sound. I didn't, did I, Gordius? Hey, hadn't we better hurry? We don't want to be left behind."

"That's just what we're going to be," his uncle told him bitterly. "Left behind. Stranded. Marooned. Abandoned."

If he'd been able to think of any more words that meant the same thing, he'd have used them, for Phaidon stared at him blankly, as if unable to understand. He gave a small smile, as if he thought his uncle was joking.

"Look at the ship," Dorian told him.

Phaidon looked and saw the oars rise and fall and the prow swing around in the clear water.

"They're going!" he said, understanding at last. "They're going without us."

"Yes."

"Cleo! They've still got Cleo!"

Uncle Pelops spread his hands. "There was nothing we could do."

Phaidon's face seemed to crack with grief and anger. He raced down into the sea, smashing up the quiet surface with his flailing arms and legs.

"Come back!" he screamed. "Come back!"

But the ship was moving steadily away. He could hear the sound of its drum above the drumming of his heart. He had no chance of catching them, however fast he swam. He pulled himself up onto a rock and shouted after them, dancing with rage, "Cleo! Cleo! I'll come and fetch you! I won't forget! You'll have your fine tomb one day! I swear to the gods, I'll find you wherever you are."

Three spears were thrown at him from the retreating ship. Two of them fell harmlessly into the sea. The third struck the rock at his feet, and he caught it up in his hand.

"Take care of her!" he shouted. "If you damage her, you'll never be safe from me! I'll kill you all if I must!"

The men of the ship looked at him but threw no more spears, either because Hiram told them not to or because the distance was too great.

II

IRIS

CHAPTER 8

To save time, they had divided the cliffs among them. The rock was not smooth. There were many ledges and cracks and holes, places for fingers and toes to cling, even shallow caves to creep into if the weather turned bad. But all the ways they tried ended in gaps too large for leaping or overhangs that only a spider could surmount. One by one they came wearily back, shaking their heads.

No. Nothing. No way out.

The sun was high in the sky. They sat in a patch of shrinking shade, hot and tired and hungry, passing around a cup of water and watching one another from under their lashes to see that nobody took more than the permitted one gulp.

When the cup was offered to Uncle Pelops, he waved it aside. "Don't waste any more water on me. Keep it for yourselves. You're young and strong. You'll survive somehow. But not me. I'm too old and fat. I'll never get out of here alive. I might as well lie down and die right now."

Dorian shrugged and passed the cup on to Phaidon.

"Nobody cares," Uncle Pelops said resentfully, not having expected to be taken at his word. "You do your best for people, but are they grateful? No. As soon as you're no more use to them, they walk off and leave you. They don't care if your bones blow about the beach like rubbish."

"You've still got a long way to go before your bones see daylight," Dorian told him. "Take your share of water or leave it, as you please, but don't play the hero. The part doesn't suit you."

Phaidon and Gordius glanced at each other but kept quiet.

It was four days since the ship had left them. Four days in which they had caught no fish in the net Hiram had given them, found no more wood for the fire, which had dwindled and gone out. They had caught only five small crabs, which they had eaten raw, and been sick as dogs all the next day. Phaidon had thrown his spear at passing seabirds and nearly succeeded in hitting his uncle's foot. Now they sat in depressed silence. Half their water and half their food had gone.

Phaidon was convinced they blamed him for everything. His shallow cut had healed cleanly. His ankle was itself again. But added to his grief for his sister was a sense of guilt. If he had kept quiet, they would be on the ship now, and Cleo would not be lost.

"I'm sorry," he said. "I know it's all my fault. If I hadn't told them about Cleo . . ."

To his surprise, they promptly disagreed with him.

Dorian said, "No, it isn't," and left it at that.

Gordius, raising his drooping head, claimed it was his fault because he'd let Cleo take in the wine to the king, because he'd been afraid. "But I'd never have let her do it if I'd known what was going to happen!" he cried. "I wouldn't! I loved her, too."

Uncle Pelops, not to be outdone, said generously, "No, no, dear boys, neither of you is to blame. It was entirely my fault. We should have stayed on Seriphos. Why should Dictys have killed us? We were only slaves. They'll still need cooks and kitchen boys and goatherds when the fighting's over. If I hadn't—um—helped myself to these few trifles, we'd have been safe enough." He shook the bag that was never far from his side and it clinked gently. "I couldn't resist their gold and silver—all because I wanted to be a free man. Free for what? To starve? To die on this dismal beach, far from home? To be eaten by crows? What a fool I was. Far better to be a well-fed slave than a free man with only stones to eat."

"No." Dorian lifted his head proudly. "I'm glad I'm free. I'll never regret it."

"Nor will I," Phaidon said eagerly, though only a moment before he'd been thinking that his uncle was right.

"Tell me that again when you're dead," Uncle Pelops said. "You were happy enough on Seriphos, my boy, laughing and playing games with the farm boys. Nessus was teaching you to play the lyre; you could have been a great singer and poet if you'd stayed there and learned the craft. Now what's to become of you? We didn't know when we were well off, that's the trouble. Why, I was like a lord in my kitchen, with other slaves under me. The king valued me. He only had me whipped the once, and though he often threw things at me, he usually missed. Only last year, when I was ill, he sent his own healer to me. Who's going to look after me now?"

"We will," they told him, a little impatiently, for he was always demanding such assurances. "We'll look after you."

He sniffed. "Very kind, I'm sure. Don't think I'm not grateful. Forgive me if I point out it's better to have a powerful king as a protector than three runaway slaves no better off than myself."

"Your king's dead. Where is his power now?" Dorian asked. "You'll—"

"There's someone up there!" Phaidon cried, jumping to his feet and pointing.

"Where?"

They all turned to look. High above their heads a ledge ran across the face of the cliff, and there, like a black shadow, was the mouth of a cave. They could see quite plainly in the sunlight the rim of rock cupping the gloomy recess. But there was nobody there.

"He was standing in the shadows," Phaidon said. "I didn't imagine it. I saw the pale shape of his face. I saw him move back when I jumped up. Come out!" he shouted, cupping his hands around his mouth. "We won't hurt you! We're friends! You don't have to be afraid of us!"

"Afraid of us . . . us . . . us," the echo mimicked.

"But do we have to be afraid of him?" Dorian muttered. "How long was he standing there? Long enough to hear what your uncle said about his—his trifles?" He nodded toward the bag Uncle Pelops was clutching nervously. "What was he like, Phaidon? Was he a big man? Armed? Was there only one?"

They all looked expectantly at Phaidon, but he could answer none of their questions. What had he seen? Only a pale blur, vaguely face-shaped, that had vanished when he looked at it.

"There was someone there," he said sulkily, sounding far from sure.

"First you hear kids laughing in the sky; now it's disappearing faces. I wasn't so far wrong when I said you were mad," his uncle grumbled, but Dorian stood up for him, saying he'd heard the laughter, too, and voices echoing on the morning Phaidon was nearly killed.

"It could well have come from up there," he said. "The figure you saw, could it have been a child's?"

"I don't know. I only saw him for a moment, and not clearly."

They called again, offering friendship, a gift of dried figs, a pretty shell Gordius had found on the beach, but only the echo of their own voices answered them.

"It's probably that spear of yours, Phaidon," Uncle Pelops said. "You should have thrown it back at the ship. It's far too big for you. You look ridiculous with it. And now it's frightened whoever it was away. It's no good saying you want to be friends when you're carrying a spear."

"I wasn't carrying it."

"You had it propped up against that rock in full view. He probably took us for a raiding party and has run back to warn his master. We'll have the whole pack of them down on us—" His voice rose in alarm. "And there's no escape." He too was on his feet now, making shuffling little runs backward and forward ı. .e an agitated dog. "No escape," he repeated piteously.

Dorian ignored him. He was staring up at the cave. "If that was a real person and not a spirit," he said, "there must be a way out through that cave. If we can get up onto that ledge . . . Let me see. Wait there."

He began walking away over the stones, stopping every now and then to study the face of the cliff, all tiredness forgotten now. They watched him and saw him leap suddenly into the air, clapping his hands like a small boy. Then he turned and shouted to them to stay where they were and wait for him. He thought he could get up on the ledge and make his way along to the cave.

"Then I'll pull you up," he said. "One by one."

It wasn't an easy climb, even for Dorian. He wound the rope around his waist, leaving both hands free. Twice his foot slipped, and he nearly fell, sending a shower of small stones rattling down the cliff.

"I'll never get up there," Uncle Pelops said dismally.

"We'll have the rope to help us. Dorian will pull us up."

"You perhaps. You're skinny. It won't bear my weight."

"It looks nearly new."

"Shoddy. It's bound to be shoddy. Like the fishing net Hiram gave us, all torn, and the grain with weevils in it. And he called himself an honest trader."

"He stole my sister," Phaidon said, "and he left us here to die. He'd better pray that he never meets me again." He picked up the spear, testing its weight in his hand, his eyes fierce.

"Do put that down, Phaidon," his uncle said nervously. "Remember what happened last time you threw it. Look, Dorian got there!"

Dorian stood gazing into the cave. Then he turned to them, put his finger to his lips, and mouthed something they couldn't understand. Next he went into the cave and disappeared from sight.

"What was all that about?" Uncle Pelops asked.

"I think he wants us to keep quiet," Gordius said.

"Why?"

"In case there's someone listening."

"Oh."

They waited for what seemed like a very long time. Phaidon began to wonder if Dorian was lying dead in the dark, robbed of his youth and strength for the jeweled dagger he wore in his belt. Perhaps Uncle Pelops was right and it was dangerous to be a free man in this wild world.

But Dorian came back, his eyes bright.

"Whoever was there has gone and left nothing behind but an odd smell," he told them. "There must be a way out, but it may not be easy to find. There are several openings leading out of the cave. . . . Come, I'll get you up here, and we'll explore together."

"Supposing we walk straight into them?" Uncle Pelops said.

Nobody asked him whom he meant by "them." They knew. He meant the strangers, the enemies, the creatures that had watched them from the cave and laughed. Perhaps they were not even human but spirits. For all they knew, they might have offended some strange island god by not offering the right sacrifice, or disturbed a sleeping monster, which now crouched somewhere out of sight. The beach, which until this moment had seemed like a trap, now looked warm and golden in the evening sunlight. Perhaps tomorrow they'd be lucky and catch some fish. Perhaps tomorrow they'd find fresh water to replenish their dwindling stock. Perhaps tomorrow a ship would come.

Dorian, untroubled by these fears, had attached one end of the rope to a jutting rock and thrown the other end down to them. "Don't worry," he called. "The rope's quite stout."

"Not as stout as I am," Uncle Pelops muttered unhappily.

"Come up first. Gordius and Phaidon can push you from behind and ease the strain. There's fresh water up here," he added to encourage them. "You can drink all you like. We'll sleep here tonight; then tomorrow we'll find the way out, and there'll be grass and trees, and goats, perhaps."

So they let him haul them up to the ledge, one by one. Uncle Pelops went first, a terrified smile on his face as Dorian pulled and sweated, and the boys thrust him up until his plump pink feet were out of their reach. Then they tied their bundles to the rope, the weevily grain and dried figs, the torn fishing net, the shrunken waterskin, and Phaidon's spear. Then Gordius. Last of all came Phaidon, swarming up the rope like a monkey and swaggering into the dark mouth of the cave before he lost his nerve.

CHAPTER 9

The day was almost over now. Sunlight had vanished from the world outside. The cave was high and gloomy, with five openings leading into the dark.

"Are we expected to crawl through those?" Uncle Pelops asked.

"They'll look better in the morning," Dorian told him, sounding so like a nurse comforting a frightened child that Phaidon blushed for his uncle, who was old enough to be the young man's father.

Uncle Pelops sniffed. He often sniffed to express a general disapproval when he couldn't decide whom to blame, but this time his nostrils quivered like a dog's. "I can smell something, the odd smell you mentioned," he said. "It's . . . no, I can't place it. What is it?"

They all sniffed. The cave smelled of wet rock from the corner where water dripped down from a crack in the stone ceiling, of seabirds' droppings and the salty tang of the sea wind blowing in,

of the dried figs and rusks Dorian was getting out for their supper
—and something else.

"I can smell it, too," Phaidon said. "A sort of indoor smell . . .
warm . . . like in the palace at night."

"You mean stuffy?" Dorian asked. "Stale food and hot bodies
and sweat?"

"No. Not that."

"Was it an animal smell?" Gordius asked. "Perhaps a lion comes
here to sleep. Or a bear. Or—" He lowered his voice. "Or something worse."

Phaidon shook his head doubtfully. The smell had gone now. He
began to wonder if he'd imagined it. He stared nervously around
the cave, peering into shadowy corners and dark openings, imagining a monster waiting out of sight, its scaly neck coiled like a rope,
its hot breath stinking—

"Perhaps it's my feet," Uncle Pelops said.

They all laughed, even Phaidon, though he knew it was not his
uncle's feet he'd smelled. It had been—smoky, a burned-out sort of
smell, like something charred. He'd smelled it before, often. It was
on the tip of his tongue, but he could not put a name to it.

"We'll keep watch again tonight and sleep near the entrance,"
Dorian told them. "If the alarm is given, run out onto the ledge, to
the left where it narrows. That way we can face them one at a time
and toss them down onto the rocks below."

They looked at him in amazement as he stood outlined against
the evening sky, so big and brave and strong, like a young giant.
Slavery had not made him soft, as it had them. "But what if they're
friendly?" Uncle Pelops asked mildly. "Don't you think we should
give them time to say welcome?"

* * *

Nothing disturbed their night. Whatever it was that haunted the island with strange sounds and smells kept away. When Dorian woke them, the cave was filling with daylight. Outside, the sun had half risen out of the sea, and the air was soft and sweet.

Not a day to be crawling about in the dark, with half a mountain over your head, Phaidon thought. He looked around and saw Gordius, sitting in the mouth of the cave, sharpening the spear on a stone.

"What are you doing? That's mine!" he cried angrily. "They threw it at me, not you. Give it to me, you thief!"

It was perhaps not the wisest way to talk to someone holding a newly sharpened spear, but Gordius only smiled and said apologetically: "Dorian told me to sharpen it."

"Oh. That's all right then. Sorry."

"He said there seem to be so many tunnels in the cliffs, like a maze, and so he thinks we should all keep together. He said the one in front should carry the spear, for obvious reasons."

"What obvious reasons?"

Gordius grinned. "Would you like someone crawling behind you in the dark with a spear pointing at your behind?" he asked.

They both laughed, and for the first time there was a warmth between them. They had been neither friends nor enemies back at home. Gordius was two years older than Phaidon, and infinitely quieter. He had worked obediently in the kitchen, but his heart hadn't been in his job, nor his appetite, for he remained as thin as a twig. Phaidon, coming back from the hills with his goats, leaping and shouting as he ran into the kitchen yard, had once surprised a look of envy on the older boy's face.

"I wonder who is going to lead the way?" he asked. "Not you or me, I bet."

"I think he meant himself," Gordius said.

They both looked across at Dorian. He had stripped and was

standing on the wet rocks beneath the crack in the ceiling of the cave, catching in his hands the water that dripped down and splashing it against his body. His wet skin gleamed gold in the cool morning light, and he looked like a god.

"It's curious, don't you think?" Gordius said softly. "There were just the three of us at first, your uncle and you and me. Dorian only came to help us with Cleo. Now she's gone, and he's taken over. He tells us all what to do, even your uncle."

Phaidon did not say anything. He was wondering where Cleo was now and whether he would ever find her again. The world seemed empty without her. First his parents had gone and now she, with not even a grave to mark their passing. *I will find her, I will,* he thought.

"I suppose someone has to be the leader," Gordius went on, "but I wish it were your uncle."

"Don't you like Dorian?" Phaidon asked.

"Mmm. I admire him. He's strong and brave and everything I'm not," Gordius said. "It's just—he can be rather hard. He'd have made a good soldier."

"Hard? I don't think he is. Look how he helped us. And he loved Cleo."

"So did I. So did all the young men," Gordius said, and added under his breath, "He'll get over it before I do."

But Phaidon had turned away and did not hear him.

It was Dorian who led them into the dark opening, the spear in his hand, dagger at his belt, and the rope tied around him and trailing behind like a rein for the others to hold. Then Uncle Pelops, his bag of treasure in one hand, the rope gripped tightly in the other. Next came Gordius, silent and frowning. Last of all was Phaidon.

"Tie the end of the rope around your waist," Dorian had instructed him. "It's darker than night in there. If you get lost, we might never find you again, and you'll end up as a fossil in the rock."

Phaidon, unlike Gordius, was not very good at knots. The rope kept slipping down over his hips and he had to keep hitching it up again. When it slipped right down to his ankles, he stepped out of it, and putting his arm through the loop, wore it over his shoulder, leaving both hands free.

The first tunnel opened out almost immediately into another cave, bigger than the one they'd just left but darker, the only light coming from the tunnel behind them. The darkness discouraged them. They had to feel their way around to make certain there were no other openings, and this took time and left their fingers sore and scraped.

The next one was blocked by a rockfall. Luckily for Dorian, the spear and not his nose hit it first. They heard the metal ring against the hard rock and thought for a moment he'd met an enemy and the fight had begun. They'd been following closely on his heels, and when he stopped abruptly, they all bumped into him in the dark, one after another. Uncle Pelops squealed, and Dorian swore at them and told them to keep their distance.

"Try to keep awake," he said irritably. "You don't have to tread on my heels. We'll have to go back."

The tunnel was narrow. There was no way he could squeeze past Uncle Pelops. They had to turn around, and Phaidon was the leader now.

"Pass me the spear, please," he said hopefully, "and the dagger."

They didn't, of course. They said he'd only trip over and cut off his own toes. They said it wasn't necessary; he could see the light at the end of the tunnel, coming from the first cave. He half hoped they'd meet a bear and it would kill them all and they'd be sorry, but nothing happened.

They reached the cave safely and sat down to recover their breath. But they could not recover their spirits. Sitting on the rock floor, they regarded the next opening gloomily, without hope.

"I hate the dark," Uncle Pelops said. "I've always hated it. If only we had a lamp."

"Well, we haven't," Dorian said shortly.

"If we had some oil," Gordius said, "we could fray pieces of the rope to make torches—"

"We haven't any oil. Or a lamp. Or anything to light one with," Dorian pointed out. "Come on, we can't sit here forever. Let's brave the dark again."

The third tunnel led steeply uphill, cold and black. On and on they went, around corner after corner, bumping their shoulders on the rock, grazing their elbows. Now and then Dorian called, "Stop!" and they shuffled to a halt behind him, while he decided which of two possible ways was the best to go. Then the rope jerked again, and they followed.

Phaidon felt the blackness lying over his face like a cloth, smelling of dust and dirt and the odd, scorched smell he could not place. He kept his hands stretched out in front of him, not wanting to bump into anything he couldn't see. His throat was dry, and his feet were sore. Once he stubbed his toe so painfully that he cried out.

"What's the matter, Phaidon?" someone asked.

"Nothing," he muttered. He was still sulking.

How odd the echoes sounded in here, so thin and high-pitched, almost like a different voice. Wasn't Echo supposed to be a girl who'd talked too much? His uncle had laughed, saying it was an old wives' tale.

His left hand suddenly lost touch with the rock wall of the tunnel. Something flickered gold and bright in the corner of his eye, and he felt a breath of air on his cheek. He turned his head sharply and found he was looking down a narrow tunnel at right angles to the one they were in, lit at the far end by a flaming torch, held in the hand of someone he could not see.

"Hey! Hello there!" he called, and the figure turned and fled. Without thinking, he dropped the rope from his shoulder and ran as fast as he could after the light. On and on, around corner after corner . . .

He was a swift runner. He had run many races back on Seriphos. But whoever held the torch was a good runner, too, a good runner but a bad loser. As he finally gained on the fleeing figure, dimly seen through the smoke and blowing sparks, the light was suddenly extinguished. He smelled again the smoky, charred smell and knew at last what it was and why it had seemed familiar: It was the smell of a torch newly put out.

With the light gone, he stumbled, tripped over his feet, and fell. He picked himself up again and stood bewildered, not knowing which way he was facing.

"Where are you?" he shouted. "Where are you?"

After the echoes died away, he thought he heard distant voices calling him, Dorian, his uncle, Gordius. But when he called again, "I'm here! I'm here!" there was no answer.

"Wait for me," he shouted, and blundered straight into solid rock, hitting his head so hard that he was sick and dizzy and had to sit down. Darkness and silence wrapped him around. He buried his face in his hands and began to cry, from fear and pain and loneliness.

Now his eyes burned. The chinks between his fingers glowed red like blood. He took his hands away from his face—and stared. At the far end of the tunnel, placed neatly in the center, was a small lamp, its flame flickering wildly in a draft he could not feel.

He got slowly to his feet and approached it cautiously. As he came nearer, he saw that the tunnel did not end in blank rock but turned sharply to the left. He stopped and held his breath, but he could hear nothing. Slowly he went forward to pick up the lamp, expecting it to be snatched away by an invisible hand or blown out by some magic, but it continued to burn.

It was made of earthenware, small and round and warm in his hands. Shielding the flame, he walked around the corner, and the light washed over the walls, picking out glittering streaks in the rock, forming a glowing bubble in which he moved. He could feel a faint draft on his face now, fresh and cool. Looking forward, he saw in front of him a pale glow, like a dim reflection, a moon to the sun he carried.

He stopped uneasily. The dim light did not move but remained steady, steadier than any living flame.

"Who's there?" he called softly, and when there was no answer, added, "I'm not armed. I'm not dangerous. I'm a friend."

Silence.

Then, out of nowhere, and also somewhat out of tune, a thin voice sang:

> I want to run and run and run
> In towns and tunnels of my own.
> I want to have my secret fun,
> I want to have my private home.
> I want to be, as I am true,
> A rat and not a friend for you.

As soon as the singing had begun, Phaidon had started creeping silently forward. The pale light grew stronger, but when he rounded the corner, there was no sign of the singer. He saw only an empty tunnel, ending in an arch of ragged rock framing the bright blue of the sky.

CHAPTER 10

It was hard to turn his back on the bright hillside and go once more into the black hole in the rock. But he must find his uncle and the others. He couldn't leave them to stumble about in the dark any longer. They wouldn't be cross with him for running off, not when they saw the light he carried. He'd be as welcome as the sun in winter.

"Uncle Pelops! Dorian! Gordius!" he called. The sound of his own voice ringing down the endless tunnels frightened him. He wondered what strange sleepers he might wake. The small flame flickered wildly, and nervous shadows cringed away as he walked. Supposing the lamp went out?

I'd go mad, he thought, *I'd howl like a wolf. I couldn't bear being lost in the dark again.*

He must have taken a wrong turning, for suddenly he found himself in a cave like no other he'd ever seen before. He stared about him with amazement, holding up the lamp. After the dark tunnel, it glowed with color. There were sheepskins and a woven blanket on a wide ledge, making a bed. A red cloak had been carelessly thrown on the floor. There were six earthenware jars of various sizes and a bronze pot holding three torches, prepared with pitch, but not lighted. In one corner stood a small charcoal brazier. He could feel the warmth of it and see the thin smoke rising toward an opening in the high ceiling of the cave, through which pale daylight seeped, silvering the curving arches of rock but leaving the floor in shadow. All around him the walls of the cave were decorated with paintings, crowding every flat space.

It was only when he looked closer that he noticed that everything was shabby and worn. The bronze pot was badly dented; the earthenware jars were cracked or chipped and, except for one half full of oil, contained nothing but a little dusty grain or mildewed fruit. The blanket and the cloak were faded and, from the look of them, had provided food for a multitude of moths.

The paintings, though childishly drawn, were vivid and strange. The one in front of him showed a large, shaggy brown animal with a ferocious smile, suckling a human baby. Below this, the artist had drawn two horizontal lines, between which a small black animal with a long, thin tail was shown running.

A rat, Phaidon thought, the unfriendly rat of the boy's song. This must be his private home. But where was he?

He turned around uneasily, suddenly convinced he was being watched. His movement made the flame of the lamp flare and shake, and dark shadows ran like rats over the floor and walls of the cave. He breathed deeply, trying to calm his racing heart. Then he called softly, "Is anyone there?"

No answer.

The boy had run from him; that did not seem warlike. He'd left him the lamp, a valuable gift at any time, but especially in the dark.

Yet he'd sung the song of the caged rat, which mothers sang to warn their children against unsuitable friendships. "A rat, and not a friend for you." Why not? Who was this boy? His possessions were old and shabby, but what slave ever owned as much? Was he a lord's son, hiding from a raiding party? Or a thief, the son of a pirate, gone to fetch his father—

Nervously Phaidon moved the lamp from side to side. Painted figures seemed to leap out from the rock, goddesses with staring eyes outlined with kohl, weird animals and birds and fishes, and here a shadowy figure, very well drawn, quite lifelike with its gleaming eyes—*eyes that blinked at the light!*

"Hey!" Phaidon shouted. Putting the lamp down quickly, he flung himself at the figure as it turned, catching it around the knees and bringing them both down hard. The stranger squealed like a pig and struggled furiously, hitting Phaidon with one hand and fumbling at his belt with the other. . . . But Phaidon had felt the cold hilt of a knife brush against his arm as they fell, and he clung with all his strength to the boy's wrists, forcing his hands apart and onto the ground.

The boy was smaller than Phaidon, and not as strong. Though at first he fought wildly, using feet and knees and teeth, he soon gave in and began sniveling. His voice was light and high, like a girl's.

"Let me go! You're hurting me!" he wailed, and burst into tears.

"Give me the knife, and I will."

"I don't trust you."

"I won't hurt you," Phaidon said. "I'm not your enemy."

"Why did you attack me then?"

Phaidon didn't know what to say. As so often, he leaped without thinking, like a cat at a shadow. He hadn't wanted the boy to run away. He'd lost his sister, his uncle, and everyone he cared for. He needed a friend. But how could he say that now, when he'd knocked the boy down and was sitting on him, pinning his wrists to the ground.

"I didn't know who you were," he mumbled. "A man almost killed me the other day. He might've come back. How was I to know? He might've murdered my uncle and my friends and come for me—"

"No. He went off on the ship. I saw him go. I've been watching you all. I saw him come creeping up to you with his knife, taking his time, like a butcher choosing the best place to cut. I got him with my first shot. Wasn't that clever?"

"You? Did you throw that stone? It was you?" Phaidon asked, staring. He let go of the boy's wrists and jumped up, keeping a wary eye on the knife. But though the boy's hand went to his belt, he did not draw the knife but merely rested his fingers lightly on the hilt.

"You saved my life," Phaidon said. "I'd be dead now but for you."

His companion smiled with obvious satisfaction. "Yes," he agreed, "you would. It's lucky for you that I'm such a good shot." Modesty did not seem to be part of his nature. "Come and sit down," he added, gesturing toward the wide ledge that served him not only as a bed and a table but as a bench as well. "Would you like some water? Or something to eat?" His eyes went doubtfully to the row of jars. "I think I have some fruit."

"I'm not hungry, thank you," Phaidon said quickly. He was looking back toward the entrance to the cave. "I wish I could stay, but I think I just heard my friends calling. They're lost down here, and I ought to find them—"

"Not yet!" the boy said quickly. "You can stay and talk. Your friends will be all right. They won't come to any harm."

"I ought to go. They're in the dark. They might fall down a hole.

They haven't got a light," Phaidon told him. His eyes went toward the lamp when he said this, but the boy was too quick for him. He snatched it up and held it to his chest, and his free hand went to his knife.

"The lamp is mine," he said.

Phaidon saw him clearly for the first time. The boy had dark, watchful eyes in a dirty face, thick black hair dimmed with dust like the bloom on grapes, and a torn and faded tunic. His arms and legs were thin and crisscrossed with scratches and tiny crescent scars. He was smaller than Phaidon, but he was fierce, a little rat with teeth.

"Come and sit down," the boy said.

Phaidon hesitated, then went with him. They sat down on the wide ledge with the lamp between them. Phaidon, who was worried that his uncle and his friends would wander off again, for he could no longer hear them, thought of snatching it up and running, but the boy was obviously waiting for him to try. He had taken the knife from his belt and was holding it to throw. He was a good shot, Phaidon remembered. He decided to sit very still, though it annoyed him to have to give way to a boy he could have beaten easily in a fair fight.

"Your name is Phaidon, isn't it?" the boy asked, in the voice of someone making polite conversation, as if he were holding the knife merely to carve his initials in the rock or clean his fingernails. "I heard them calling you on the beach. And the fat man's your uncle. Uncle Pelops. Pelops is a funny name, isn't it?"

Phaidon didn't answer.

"Don't sulk. The other two, the big man and the thin boy, are they your brothers?"

"They're friends."

"Who's Cleo?"

"How did you hear of her?" Phaidon cried. "Who talked of her? What did they say?"

"Nothing much," the other said, startled. "What's the matter? I heard you shout her name when the ship left, that's all. You said you'd come for her." He paused, but went on when Phaidon said nothing. "Who is she?"

"My sister," Phaidon said, and turned his face away.

"Did they take her with them? I'm sorry."

There was a long silence. Then the boy said softly, half to himself, "I wanted there to be a girl. If I'd known she was on the ship, I'd have swum out to it. I can swim, you know. Not many people can, not even sailors. I'd have swum out with my knife in my teeth, and I'd have cut the throat of anyone who'd tried to stop me. I'd have rescued her."

Phaidon still did not say anything. He knew if he tried to speak, he would cry. He thought of the huge men the captain had left on board to guard the ship. He thought of his poor stone sister in the hold, unable to run, too heavy to lift, she who had been such a pretty dancer. He wished he could dream such silly dreams of triumph, but Cleo was dead.

"I saw your ship come in and watched the men jumping off like fleas," the other went on. "I hoped . . . But there weren't any women or girls with them. I'd thought they might be a raiding party, you see. Sometimes they carry women and girls with them, to sell as slaves, but I couldn't see any. If I'd known there was a girl hidden on the ship, I'd have got her away somehow. She could have lived here with me. I'd have shared everything with her."

Phaidon looked at him curiously. "You're a bit young to get married," he said, laughing.

"You don't understand. You never asked my name, did you? It's Iris."

"Irus?"

"No. *Iris*," she said, stressing the ending.

"That's a girl's name!"

"I know. I am a girl. You didn't guess, did you?"

Phaidon stared. Could he be a girl? This fierce, dirty, ragged creature was nothing like his pretty sister, nothing like the girls on Seriphos, who were soft and laughing and wore bright ribbons to tie back their curls. Yet his voice was high, and for all his ferocity, he had little strength. Yes, he—she could be a girl.

"Why do you dress like a boy and cut your hair short?" he asked.

"I'm growing up," she said, shrugging her shoulders. "I have to be careful. I haven't a mother or father to look after me now. There's nobody. And I didn't like the look of those men. It's safer sometimes to be a boy. What's the matter?"

"I thought I heard them again," Phaidon said, going to the mouth of the tunnel. "I thought I heard my friends calling me." He listened, but there was nothing, except the sound of water dripping somewhere. "I hope nothing's happened to them."

Suddenly, from behind him, he heard something crackle and smelled again the familiar smell of burning pitch. He turned and saw the girl holding out a flaring torch to him.

"Take it and go!" she said angrily. "Go on, you know you want to. Your feet are itching to run off. A torch is better than a lamp if you are running. It won't blow out. Go on!"

He took it from her. "I'll come back, I promise," he said.

"You won't. That's what my father said, 'I'll come back. I promise,' but he didn't. I don't care. I didn't need him. I don't need anybody. Go on!"

He hesitated, looking back at her as she stood in the cave she had tried to make into a home, with its painted walls and bed of sheepskins and the empty jars of food in a row. The smoke from the torch curled around her head like gray snakes, but her eyes were nothing like the terrible, cold eyes of the Gorgon. They were the frightened eyes of a child.

"Come with me," he said, holding out his hand to her. "Uncle Pelops won't mind one more. Five is a better number than four. Besides," he added with a teasing smile, "you're a rich girl. You've a lamp and oil to burn in it. They'll be overjoyed to see you after being so long in the dark."

CHAPTER 11

They sat around a small fire in the late-afternoon sunlight, with the smell of their first hot supper in days making their mouths water. The island was called Kapnos, the girl told them. It looked beautiful to them after the dark tunnel, even the scrubby grass, full of thistles and thorns.

"A lovely, lovely place," Uncle Pelops said, beaming at Iris.

Phaidon had been right. Any girl who brought a light and led them out into the fresh air was more than welcome—even if, to be honest, she was a little peculiar, dressed as a boy and very dirty. After all, they were themselves a pretty villainous-looking lot now, as ragged and dirty as she was. She'd been frightened when she'd first met them in the tunnels and might have run away if Phaidon had not been close behind her.

Now she looked at Uncle Pelops as if he were mad and told him that Kapnos was small and horrible. Nothing lived on it except lizards and birds. Besides, it was dangerous.

"I wish we could get away," she said. "I wish we could get to the mainland."

"How far is the mainland from here?" Dorian asked.

"Six deaths away," she muttered.

They stared at her, puzzled, and asked her what she meant, but she said she didn't want to talk about it. Later. Not now. It was too terrible. It would only put them off their food.

There was no doubt she was odd, but they owed her too much to be critical. She had shared all she had with them: her lamp, her torches, her oil. It was her dried fish they were cooking in her bronze pot, her sheepskins they sat on. All this she'd given and asked for nothing in return. But she must want something.

Us, Phaidon thought. *She's lonely. She wants to belong to somebody.* "I wish we could get to the mainland," she'd said, not "I wish I could." Well, that was all right. He wanted to get to the mainland, too.

But Uncle Pelops said he'd had enough of the sea. "We might do worse than settle here," he suggested. "A farm perhaps . . ."

"Here? Nothing grows here. Only a few firs and stunted bushes," Iris told him. "Even the grass is as thin as an old man's hair. Look at it! There's hardly enough to feed one sheep, let alone a flock. And see that mountain?" She turned and pointed to the odd-shaped mountain, steep-sided and flat-topped, that dominated the view. "That's a volcano. My father said one day fire will shoot out of the top and burn up all the stars, and there'll be nothing left of Kapnos."

"Oh, dear," Uncle Pelops said, leaning forward to stir the fish stew. "Did he say when this was likely to happen? Not before we've had supper, I hope?"

It was obvious that he did not believe in exploding mountains, but Dorian looked thoughtful and said he'd heard of such things.

"Yes, yes, travelers' tales," Uncle Pelops said scornfully. He seemed to have forgotten that at least one traveler's tale had turned out to be true. "Nobody would live here if he were likely to be burned up at any moment—"

"Nobody does live here," she told him. "Nobody ever comes here, except as you came, by accident, blown by a tempest."

They looked at her unhappily. They'd imagined, if not a palace, there would be at least a village or two, and farms, somewhere for them to go when they'd finished their fish stew and tidied themselves up as best they could. A bed for the night and with luck a welcome for four weary travelers.

"You mean the four of us are the only people on the whole island?" Uncle Pelops asked.

"The five of us," she said.

"Yes, of course, five counting you. How did you come? You can't have come all by yourself? And all the things in your cave . . . There must have been other people with you. Where did you come from?"

She leaned forward, more than willing to tell them her story. Her very eagerness to talk began to convince them that she had indeed been alone for a long time, with no one to listen to her. She told them that she and her father came from a small village on the mainland, near the palace of Sparta. Her father, well, he wasn't her father really, he'd found her in a bear's cave up in the mountains when she was little more than a baby—

"In a bear's cave?"

"Yes. The bear wasn't there at the time. She'd gone hunting for food for us, me and my brother. I mean, her other cub," Iris said firmly, daring them to disbelieve her. "My father never saw the mother bear, but he said her footprints were in the dust all around us."

"You mean a real bear, one with shaggy fur and four feet and round ears?" Uncle Pelops asked, wanting to be sure there was no misunderstanding.

"Yes," she said, scowling, guessing he didn't believe her, "a she-bear. My father, I mean, Marmax, the man who found me, said I must have been left out on the mountain as a gift for the gods. He said it was often done after a bad harvest, when there were too many children already and too little food to go around. He said it was fair enough. First come, first served, he said."

"Well, you'll be first served here," Uncle Pelops told her warmly, "even if you are last come." Although he couldn't swallow the she-bear, he could easily believe that she was an abandoned child. She had an uncared-for look. And he had always been a big softhead where unhappy children were concerned. Look how he'd adopted Cleo and Phaidon, who were, in fact, no kin of his but had been found lost and crying in the ashes of their burned village.

He had poured the fish stew into a large, shallow silver dish to cool and now pushed it toward her, telling her to help herself first. "Don't burn your fingers," he warned her.

"How come the bear didn't eat you?" Phaidon asked, watching her hungrily as she chose the biggest lump of fish.

"I don't know. She'd just had one cub; perhaps she thought I was a second one. Anyway, she suckled us both. When Marmax found me, the cub and I were playing together. He thought the cub was attacking me and grabbed his knife, meaning to kill it. This knife— She touched the one in her belt. "But I growled at him and bit his ankle. He said I went for him every time he tried to get hold of the bear cub; he'd never seen anything like it. So in the end he left it alone for its mother to find. Me, he wrapped in his cloak and took home with him, though he had no wife to look after me. The people in his village said he was mad and that I was no better than a wild animal. Though I looked to be about two or three years old, I could neither talk nor walk upright but only growled and scratched and ran about on all fours. You can still see the scars—or you could if my knees were cleaner."

She leaned forward and spat on one of her knees and rubbed the dirt away with her hand. "See, those were from sharp stones, and these on my arms and legs are from my brother, the cub, I mean, when we played together. He used to nip me. He couldn't seem to get used to my having no fur to protect me."

They'd been listening to her silently, not believing a word she said, but this last part was oddly convincing.

"How can you remember it if you were so young?" Phaidon asked doubtfully.

"I can't, not really. It's what my father told me, and the people in the village. But sometimes, when I was warm and half asleep, with one of the dogs curled up beside me, I'd think I was back. . . . But it was probably only a dream."

She had never gone back to the cave in the mountains, she told them. She had wanted to, but her father had told her the bears would not recognize her and would probably kill her. He'd made her promise she wouldn't ever go, and she'd kept her promise because he was kind to her and called her his daughter.

"His servants looked after me when he was at sea," she said. "And I was going to look after him when he was old, as he had no family. His hair was already going gray. I didn't want him to go to sea anymore. It's too dangerous, but he said how could we live otherwise?"

"Was he a fisherman?" Uncle Pelops asked, reaching forward to help himself from the silver dish.

"No," she said.

Phaidon remembered all the things in her cave, the storage jars, the lamp and the bronze pot, the blankets and sheepskins. "Was he a merchant?" he asked.

"No! What does it matter what he was?" she demanded angrily. "What's it got to do with you?"

He could not understand why she was suddenly so angry. She had told them such an extraordinary tale so readily, why refuse to tell them what her father did? She'd sounded almost proud of having a bear as a foster mother; what on earth could her father be to make her ashamed to say?

Then he guessed. "Was he a pirate?" he asked.

"Supposing he was? He had to live, didn't he? He was kind to me. None of the other people in the village wanted me. They'd have thrown me out if they'd had their way. He saved my life."

Phaidon did not want to look at her. He gazed down at his hands and saw that they were trembling. He clenched his fists. There were hundreds of pirates, infesting the seas like sharks. It was hardly likely to have been her father who had come on that day, long ago, when his mother had sent him and Cleo to hide in the woods. The smell of smoke from the fire brought back the memory fresh, the noise of shouting, the flames crackling, and the screams. Cleo had held him tight in her arms and whispered to him to keep quiet. "It's a game," she'd said, "a game of hide-and-seek. Mommy will come and find us when the bad men have gone."

But nobody had come to find them. They'd stayed in the woods till it was dark and the smoke from their burning village obscured the moon.

It's not the girl's fault, he told himself, but he never wanted to see her again. Even the sound of her voice was hateful to him now.

She was saying that her father had been taking her to Lassa, to stay with some friends of his while he was away. He'd been going to take her overland, but as usual she had begged for a ride in the boat, and as usual he'd given in.

"Perhaps I brought them bad luck," she said. "There was a terrible storm, and we were blown right out of our way. We—we lost six of our crew. . . ." Her voice shook, and she muttered something about it being horrible, horrible.

Then she went on to say that the rest of them had struggled with the oars and more by luck than judgment had avoided the rocks and landed their boat in a small, sandy bay on the other side of Kapnos.

"You mean, they're there now?" Dorian asked, sitting up, but she shook her head and told him they'd stayed only a week or two, to unload the boat and explore.

"Then they left me here while they set out to see if there were any better islands nearby," she said. "I begged my father not to go, but he said he must. He said he'd come back for me, but he never did. None of them came back. I saw the boat drifting in early one morning and went running out to meet it. It was bumping and scraping its sides against the rocks. I knew there was something wrong. When I reached it, I saw it was empty, except for their cloaks rolled up underneath the benches and my father's knife lying in the bottom. This knife. He'd never have left it. He'd had it since he was a boy. I knew as soon as I saw it that he must be dead."

She began to cry.

Phaidon looked up. Uncle Pelops was hugging her and stroking her rough hair. Gordius handed her a cup of wine, and Dorian patted her arm.

He did not move. Her tears confused him. She was weeping for the pirate who'd been like a father to her. She was weeping for a man who'd robbed and burned and killed, who might, perhaps, have been the one who'd killed his own parents, that day long ago. What sort of girl was this, who cried for a murderer? And what sort of boy was he, to feel sorry for her, instead of vowing revenge?

CHAPTER 12

There was no doubt, Uncle Pelops and Dorian agreed, that Phaidon's new friend was something of a little liar. Suckled by a bear, indeed!

"She's not my friend. I just met her in the caves," Phaidon said, and saw Dorian frown with disapproval, as if he thought he'd been disloyal. "Just because I saw her before you did doesn't mean she's mine. I can't be friends with the daughter of a pirate!" he cried hotly.

"That may not be true either," Uncle Pelops said. "Poor boy, try not to let it upset you. I expect she made the whole thing up."

But some of what she said turned out to be true. The boat was there, rocking gently in the shallows of a small bay on the west side of the island. She led them there the next morning, a rough walk across the side of the mountain, not a walk to attempt by moonlight unless you wanted to break your leg.

They set out as soon as the sun was up, stumbling after her as she raced ahead, as nimble as a goat. The bay, when they reached it, looked like a shallow dish, half filled with a pale, gritty sand and rimmed with low, broken cliffs. Odd currents rumpled the bright surface of the sea, sending small waves to lick the sides of the boat.

It was no ordinary little fishing boat, but a well-built galley, large enough for a crew of twenty men. They waded out to it. Looking inside, they saw that though there were sixteen rowlocks, there were only three oars lying next to the lowered mast and furled sail in the bottom of the boat. Nothing else. No rolled-up cloaks or bundles beneath the benches, no storage jars or waterskins, not even the usual litter of orange peel and apple cores in the bilge water. The inside of the boat was as clean as a new hut. Only the polished patches on the wooden benches showed that men had once sat there, plying the missing oars. A single rope attached it to a boulder on the shore.

There was something eerie about the gently rocking boat, so clean and so empty, its sides scarcely scratched by its passage through the rocks in the bay. Who would abandon a valuable boat like this? They looked around uneasily, expecting pirates to come leaping out from behind the boulders and bushes, shouting and waving their hot swords in the sun.

But nothing stirred on the shore. There was no sound but the crying of the gulls and the faint lapping of water against the sides of the boat.

"I don't understand," Dorian said, keeping his voice down for fear of hidden listeners, "where have they gone? How could the boat come here by itself? It'd have been dashed to pieces on the rocks in the storm."

"There was no storm then," the girl insisted. "It was a clear, still day when it drifted in. I saw it from the top of the cliffs up there.

The current brought it in. It must've spun out from the edge of the whirlpool—"

"Whirlpool? What whirlpool?" Uncle Pelops asked.

"Out there!" she said, pointing vaguely to the sea. "They'd meant to skirt around it to the left, to avoid having to pass the monster again, but they had to keep out—there are sharp rocks on that side—and the current swung them around and carried them back the way we came. I thought the whirlpool would get them, but they managed to row clear, even though they were six men short. When they were out of sight, I knelt on the sand and prayed to the gods to save my father from the monster. But he never came back. None of them came back."

Her face crumpled. Turning away abruptly, she splashed her way back to the shore, kicking at the sea as if to punish it for all the deaths it caused. They looked after her in silence.

Then Gordius asked, his eyes wide and frightened, "Monster? Does she mean here? On this island?"

"Really, Gordius, dear boy, monsters? Surely no sensible person can believe in—" Uncle Pelops broke off, catching Phaidon looking at him.

"I suppose there may well be many strange creatures in the world that we've never come across," Dorian said mildly. "Take the camel, for example. Now that sounds to be a peculiar beast. Yet I met a man from Egypt who said they ride them there like horses."

"I don't pretend to be a great traveler myself," Uncle Pelops remarked, "but I'll be very surprised if that girl's monster turns out to be anything more terrible than—than a large dog."

Dorian smiled, and Gordius looked relieved, but Phaidon had seen the terror in Iris's eyes when she'd mentioned the monster, and he could not help believing her. However, he said nothing and merely smiled with the rest, not wanting Dorian to think him a fool.

"Poor girl," Uncle Pelops said, looking across to Iris, who was now lying facedownward on the sand. "We must be kind to her. Go and comfort her, Phaidon, while we three run the boat up on the sand. I don't trust this rope. It's very worn."

Phaidon did not want to comfort Iris. He was not sorry that her pirate father was dead and didn't want to have to pretend he was.

"It's a heavy boat," he said. "You'll need me to help push."

His uncle ordered him irritably to do what he was told, while Dorian laughed and said, "I think we can manage without you, shrimp, thank you all the same."

Phaidon waded angrily back to the beach and sat down beside Iris, though not close enough to be expected to pat her shoulder or hold her hand. She was lying with her face turned away from him, and she did not look up or say anything. Her legs had been washed clean by the sea, and the small, pale scars showed up clearly against her brown skin. They could be bites, he thought, the playful bites of a bear cub. Everything she told them might be true, just as the head of the Gorgon had been true.

"What was the monster like?" he asked.

She didn't answer, and he looked away from her to the boat. He was glad to see they were having trouble getting it beached. Every time they tried to run it in on a wave, it stuck on the edge of the sea, churning up the sand and dirtying the white foam.

"He's not as strong as he thinks," he said.

"Who?" Iris asked, sitting up. She had been crying; her face was all smudged.

"Dorian," he told her.

"I thought you liked him," she said. "I thought he was your hero."

"I do like him. It's just . . ." He hesitated and then admitted ruefully, "He always makes me feel small. He doesn't mean to, but —I suppose he doesn't think much of me. I think he likes Gordius better than me."

"I don't," she said. "I like you best. Shall I take you to see the whirlpool? You can see it from up on those cliffs."

He'd never seen a whirlpool before and went with her eagerly. They clambered up the narrow path they'd come down that morning and then up a steep, grassy slope until they reached the highest point overlooking the sea. Down below, in the bay, he saw the tiny figures of Uncle Pelops and Dorian and Gordius still struggling in vain with the boat.

"Look over there!" the girl said, pointing. "Over to the right. By those two crags, see it?"

He shielded his eyes with his hands. He did not know which two crags she meant; there were rocks everywhere, thrusting their wet dark heads out of the water like giant dogs. Then, farther out than he had expected, he saw a strange elliptical disturbance, a rushing and spinning of dark water, throwing up specks of white foam like spittle from an old man's mouth.

"See the dark hole in the center?" Iris said. "If you listen carefully, you can just hear the roar it gives as it swallows down sea and ships and fish into its mouth and grinds them up into splinters of wood and bone and blood, before it vomits them out again. See that tall, dark crag sticking up behind those cliffs? That's where the monster lives."

Phaidon stared at the pinnacle of black rock that rose up to pierce the sky. Clouds bled from its tip, staining the blue air around it.

"That's the way back to the mainland," she said. "That's the way we'd have to go. There isn't any other."

"Can't we kill the monster?"

"We wouldn't stand a chance. We had twelve men when we set out, twelve men armed with bows and swords and spears, men used to fighting. We'd been warned about the monster, but we thought we were a match for anything that lived. We'd come to two crags, they told us, one with a crooked fir tree leaning out over the whirlpool and the other in which the monster lived, in a cave so high that our spears and arrows couldn't reach her but fell uselessly into the sea."

"If the cave is so high, how did she reach you? Can she fly?"

"No. She never leaves her cave. They told us she could not, her foul body was too bloated. . . . But she does not need to leave it. She has six heads, each on the end on a long neck, like a snake. I saw them! I saw them uncoiling above us. It was horrible, horrible!" She drew in a long, sobbing breath, bit her knuckles hard, and then went on more quietly. "There was nothing we could do to escape. Our men were forced to row for their lives to avoid the whirlpool that sucked and pulled at our boat, while she, safe in the air above us, had time to take her pick, like a fat lady choosing sweets out of a dish. Six of our men she took. I heard them scream."

She put her hands over her ears to shut the sound out, but the screams were inside her own head. Phaidon put his arm around her and felt her shivering in the hot sunlight. He forgot to worry about what her father had been but thought only of comforting her. When he looked back at the whirlpool and the tall crag, he felt in need of comfort, too.

CHAPTER 13

"Six heads?" Uncle Pelops asked.

"Yes," Iris replied, meeting his eyes boldly.

"And only one body?"

"So they told us."

"I thought you said you'd seen the monster yourself," Dorian put in, frowning.

Phaidon and Iris had come down from the headland and found the others sitting in the shade of some crooked firs, resting after their futile labor with the boat, which still floated in the shallows, exactly as they had found it. They had listened in silence while Iris retold her story, an irritable silence, like people who have better things to do than listen to childish tales.

"I only saw it for a moment," Iris explained. "Its shadow fell across the boat. I looked up, and there it was—all necks and heads, necks and heads dark against the sky. Then my father pushed me into the bottom of the boat and threw his cloak over me. I didn't see any more. But I heard the men scream."

And to every further question, her answer was: "I didn't notice. . . . I was too frightened. . . . It all happened so quickly." At last, shaming their doubts, she cried, "I did see it! I did! I have nightmares every night!"

So they went up with her to the headland and looked gloomily at the distant pattern of the whirlpool spinning on the shaken sea and the tall crag where she claimed the monster lived.

"Are you telling us that there's no safe way out of this bay?" Dorian asked. "No safe way to reach the mainland?"

"Not without losing six out of the boat."

"That's hardly encouraging, seeing there are only five of us," Uncle Pelops said. "You're joking, aren't you, dear child? Come, you can tell me. I won't be angry with you."

"I'm telling the truth," she said.

They did not want to believe her. They wanted to leave this island. She had been right about it; it was a barren, lonely place. Everything on it, the stunted firs, the twisted bushes, and the tiny flowers, had a starved look. Even Uncle Pelops dwindled in the sun, his fat face collapsing into hanging jowls.

They were used to getting their food from markets and farms. Iris was the only one who was good at hunting. They began to think she might after all have been raised by a bear. She could catch fish in her hands. She knew where to find crabs' and turtles' eggs. She climbed the cliffs to rob the seabirds' nests, showed them how to lay traps for rats and voles, and warned them which plants were poisonous: "Beware of spotted leaves; be careful of fungi." But for all her skill, there were days when their stews consisted of little but water and weeds and days when an unlucky ingredient made them all sick.

Yet Phaidon was oddly happy. The warm days were too busy and he was too young for constant grief. Hours passed without his thinking of poor Cleo. His skill was improving. Soon he was able to hit the trunk of a dead tree with his spear six times out of ten. One morning he caught a fish in his hands, so surprising himself that he let it slip through his fingers back into the sea. Iris laughed and told him he would make a good hunter one day if he didn't starve first.

In the afternoons they collected the driftwood that littered the rocks on this side of the island, remnants of unlucky ships that had failed to find shelter from the storms. Every evening Dorian, back from his solitary tramps, would sort through the growing pile to find a piece long enough to suit him and would sit, whittling it with his dagger, while Iris watched him, her dark eyes glinting in the firelight.

"What's that meant to be?" she asked one night.

"An oar for the boat," he said, a little defensively, for it was indeed an odd shape, the plank he was making it from having had a decided curve.

"There are three already in the boat," she told him.

"We'll need more than that."

"There's the sail."

"I know. I saw it. But without enough oars, we'd be at the mercy of the wind, and none of us are experienced sailors. Unless perhaps you are?" he added, with the smile of someone humoring a small child.

"Yes, I am," she said, tossing her head. "My father taught me. He was their steersman. He showed me how to do it. It takes great skill and sharp eyes. You have to have a feel for it. Not everyone can do it. My father was very good. He could've steered a course through a dog's snapping teeth and never shown a scratch. It wasn't his fault the current carried them the wrong way. He warned the captain it wasn't safe, but the captain would go. That's why he left me behind. He knew they'd never make it."

Dorian put the oar down and stared out to sea.

"There isn't any other way out," he said at last. "I've been all over the island, but I can't find another possible place to launch a boat, only high cliffs and crags and rocks as sharp as knives. Even if we could find a way to move the boat any distance, there's no way we could lower it safely into the sea. Our ropes are too short."

"That's what we found," Iris said. "Our men spent weeks looking but found nowhere any good. I'd have told you so, but I didn't think you'd believe me. You'd have wanted to see for yourself. Our men even thought of taking the boat to pieces, small enough to carry through the caves and tunnels leading to your bay. But none of them were sure they could put it together again, not without the proper tools. We had no skilled craftsmen with us for a job like that."

"And neither have we," Uncle Pelops said hastily, seeing Dorian look interested. "I wouldn't try it, my dear fellow, really I wouldn't. We don't want to ruin the boat. Think how useful it will be for fishing in the bay, when Gordius has finished mending the net with his clever fingers. As long as we stay within—"

"Stay! I don't want to stay!" Dorian cried passionately, surprising them all, for he was usually even-tempered. He sprang to his feet, walked a few paces away, and stood with his back to them, staring out to sea. "I'd rather die than rot on this barren island. Who knows how long we may have to wait until another ship comes? If one ever does. I'm a young man. I want to drink with my friends and dance with the girls, not wither away here like those miserable trees. No, as soon as I'm ready, I'll take my chance. You can come with me or stay here, as you wish, but I'm taking the boat."

"It doesn't belong to you," Iris muttered, half under her breath, for she was a little afraid of Dorian.

He heard her, however, and, coming back to them, said fiercely, "The boat belongs to whoever has the courage to put to sea. Who will come with me?"

They were silent, staring at him as if he'd gone mad.

"None of you, it seems," Dorian said bitterly, turning from them.

"I will! I will come!" Phaidon cried.

His uncle, of course, would not hear of it. He absolutely forbade it. They must wait. They must think. There was no point in rushing into things. How could a man and a boy handle a boat meant for a crew of eighteen to twenty men?

"You forget the sail. The sail is sound, I had a look at it. We'd wait for a good wind before we started, and then with luck, and the help of the gods, the two of us might manage——Dorian caught sight of Phaidon's face, both excited and frightened and very young. He smiled ruefully and said, "I suppose we wouldn't have much hope. . . . Three would be better."

"Don't look at me. I'm not coming with you," Iris said. "I don't want to die yet. Not now, when all summer's ahead. Don't go, Phaidon. It'll be easier here in the summer. We won't go hungry then. And a ship may come."

Gordius, as usual, said nothing but bent over the net he was mending, curving his back like a crab retreating into its shell.

Dorian shrugged and walked off across the sand to stand at the edge of the sea, looking at the boat. Phaidon followed him.

"It's all right, Dorian," he said. "I'm sure we can manage somehow. With a little luck."

"A little luck? I wish that were all we needed. Your uncle is right, Phaidon; it was a mad idea. It'd be just throwing your life away."

"You think I'm too young, don't you?"

Dorian looked down at him and smiled. "Yes, I do think you're too young. Too young to waste your life. Don't worry, it's something you'll grow out of, given time."

"Don't laugh at me!"

"I'm sorry. I didn't mean— Look, go back to your uncle, there's a good boy. I'm not in the mood for company just now."

Phaidon hesitated. Then he said, "Don't go by yourself, Dorian. Promise me you won't go by yourself, not without giving me a chance to come. I can't stay here forever. I have to find Cleo. I made a vow I have to keep. I swore to the gods I'd give her a proper burial, and I will."

Dorian was silent for so long that Phaidon thought he was not going to answer. At last he said, "Are you trying to shame me because I spoke of dancing with other girls? I've not forgotten Cleo; I never will. But I'm a young man, Phaidon, and I'll want to marry some other girl one day. Try not to blame me too much. You're too young to understand now. . . ."

"No, I'm not," Phaidon told him. "I don't blame you. Take me with you."

"I promise I won't go without letting you know first. I can't promise to take you with me, not unless your uncle agrees. How could I? It would be almost as bad as murder."

The following evening, after they had eaten, Phaidon went up to the headland by himself and watched the sun sink down to touch the sea, staining it red as if with blood. Down below him on the beach Uncle Pelops and Dorian were still arguing, though he could not hear what they said. He sighed and looked over to the crag where the monster lived, standing dark against the flaming sky. He could not help wishing he hadn't told Dorian that he wanted to go, but it was too late to change his mind.

He knew he could get around his uncle. He always had done so before, when he really tried hard. Uncle Pelops could sound fierce, but he was soft inside. . . . Dorian might not know that. Dorian probably believed his uncle would never agree to his going. . . . No. It wouldn't be honorable not to do his best to persuade him. He'd always remember he'd been afraid.

To stop himself from dwelling on these gloomy thoughts, he began making up a song in his mind, as he often did, to distract himself from his troubles. He gave it a jaunty, bouncing tune, but the monster overshadowed his thoughts and invaded the words:

> *A monster with so many heads,*
> *Necks and heads, necks and heads,*
> *Frightens children in their beds,*
> *Rips the quiet night to shreds*
> *As they scream for mommy.*
>
> *A monster with so many necks,*
> *Heads and necks, heads and necks,*
> *Must the waking mind perplex.*
> *How can a creature so complex*
> *Possess a single tummy?*

Gordius, coming up unnoticed, his feet silent on the scrubby grass of the headland, listened with amazement to the high, sweet voice ringing out into the darkening sky and wondered how anyone could make a jest of so ghastly a creature and the grim fate that might well await him if he went with Dorian. He wished he had Phaidon's courage. He didn't know it was mostly bravado.

Phaidon was still singing:

> *And if of us it eats its fill,*
> *Crunch and kill, crunch and kill,*
> *I hope its greed will make it ill,*
> *And we brave sailors overspill*
> *Its equilibrium-mee!*

"I think you mean 'equilibrium,' not 'equilibriummy,' " Gordius said.

Phaidon looked around, rather peeved at having been overheard. "I know," he said. "But it wouldn't rhyme, would it? What do you want?"

Gordius winced at his ungracious tone but sat down beside him.

"I want to talk to you, to see what you think before I tell them. If you think it's worth telling them . . . I had this idea, you see," he said. "I got it from something Iris told us about the monster. You remember how she said that it always takes six out of any boat, but no more because by then the boat would be out of reach— unless, of course, it overturned."

"What does it matter?" Phaidon asked impatiently. "There'll only be two of us. Even if we all go, there'd only be five."

"We could make six more." Gordius leaned forward eagerly. "Six dummies, with round heads like puddings tied up in cloth. Iris can paint faces on them, and we could each cut some of our hair off for them. We're all getting as shaggy as ill-kempt dogs. We could stuff all the cloaks with dried grass and leaves and rubbish, and fasten them onto the benches so that they look like oarsmen, bigger and more worth eating than we are. Perhaps we could choose a misty day when the monster won't be able to see clearly. What do you think, Phaidon?"

"I think you're a genius," Phaidon said, his eyes shining. "I don't see why it shouldn't work. We could duck down at the last minute and let the boat sail by, with only the six dummies showing above the benches. We could all go, then, even Uncle Pelops. You're brilliant, Gordius. Let's go and tell them!"

Gordius laughed with pleasure, and they ran down to the beach together, singing joyfully, "Heads and necks!" at the tops of their voices.

CHAPTER 14

Gordius told the others of his plan that night, when a cold wind was blowing off the sea and the fire was smoking sulkily. Perhaps he had chosen the wrong moment. Neither of the men was impressed.

"Do you really think the monster, if there is one, which I doubt, would prefer a grass dummy to me?" Uncle Pelops asked, with a short, coughing laugh. "I may have lost weight but there's still plenty of good meat on me. I'd be the first to go."

Dorian, too, didn't seem to think that the idea would work, though he said with careless kindness that there was no harm in trying, if they wanted something to do in the evenings. But not with his cloak, thank you. It was not summer yet. The nights were still cold.

"I suppose it was a stupid idea," Gordius muttered when the two men had gone off to find somewhere to sleep out of the path of the smoke.

"No, it's not. It's an excellent idea. They speak as if we're children, wanting to play with dolls. Just because you thought of it and not them, they think it can't be any good," Phaidon said angrily.

But they had won somebody over to their side. They had forgotten Iris and jumped when her voice came out of the dark, so close that they could feel her breath on their cheeks.

"Let's show them," she whispered. "We don't need their cloaks. Come with me to the caves tomorrow and see what I've got hidden away. Eight cloaks and eight bundles. I told you they were still under the benches when the boat came back. I took them out for safekeeping and hid them high up on a ledge in my cave. I wondered why you didn't ask me about them. But then, you never seem to believe half I say."

This was so true that they did not know how to answer her.

"We'll leave early before they're awake," she went on. "I don't want Dorian to come with us. He's already taken over their boat. I don't want him to have their bundles as well. They're not his. If they're anybody's, they're mine. My inheritance. But I don't mind sharing it with you, Phaidon."

"And with Gordius. It was his idea," Phaidon said, seeing the other boy smile. He had already been teased by his uncle and Dorian about the wild girl's obvious preference for him. He did not want Gordius to start. "We'll share it between us," he said.

"But I get first pick," she said sharply, half regretting her generosity.

"What's in the bundles?" Gordius asked.

She told them she did not know. She hadn't opened them. "I kept thinking they'd come back one day, and the captain would whip me if I touched anything of theirs. But they won't come back now, will they? They won't come back out of the sea?"

"No. I don't think they'll ever come back," Gordius said gently.

"They're dead," she agreed, as if she'd known it all along, from the time she'd seen her father's knife in the bottom of the boat. After a pause she added, "I didn't like the captain. He had a terrible temper. I'm not sorry about him. I wonder what he's got in his bundle. It's very heavy. Perhaps it's gold."

But it was golden honey, not the metal, that weighed down the captain's bundle, golden honey for his sweet tooth, and a small leather bag of silver nuggets, useful for trading.

"That's mine," Iris said, taking the bag quickly, as if she did not trust them not to grab. "Your uncle can have the honey for his cooking, and look, here's another knife. . . ."

They had left the sandy bay early that morning, before the sun was properly up, and were now sitting outside the caves, with the contents of the bundles spread out before them on the ground, like a street market in which everything was free, or a king's birthday.

There were cloaks and blankets, leather jerkins and other garments of all different sizes and colors, jars of sugared plums and nuts, sacks of corn and dried apricots and figs. There were three knives in leather sheaths and a bronze ax. There were trinkets: silver combs for a lady's hair, bronze buckles for men's cloaks, and a delicate circle of coral and silver and blue glass beads, originally intended for a nobleman's lady and now fastened around the thin brown neck of a pirate's adopted daughter.

"How do I look?" she asked, laughing.

She looked better, there was no doubt about it. The sea had washed her more or less clean, and her hair, though still short and untidy, curled softly around her small ears. The bright circlet on her neck suited her and made her dark eyes sparkle.

"Fine," Phaidon said.

"Like a lady?"

A lady in a ragged boy's tunic, with skinny arms and legs crisscrossed with old scars? He looked down to hide the amusement in his eyes, for she had a quick temper. Bending over to pick up a small copper bracelet, he pretended a sudden interest in it, leaving Gordius to make the tactful answer.

It was a child's bracelet, too small to fit around even his thin wrist. Not a rich man's child, or it would have been more elaborate. A thin copper band such as he'd often seen on the dimpled wrists of babies in his own village. A copper bracelet to bring good luck and protect its wearer from harm.

His hand began to shake. He seemed to hear again the sound of shouting and to see the red smoke come drifting through the trees as his village burned. His village or another, it made no difference. He wanted no part of these spoils. This little bracelet had brought no luck, but only killers out of the sea.

"What happened to the baby who wore this?" he shouted, leaping to his feet. "What happened to the woman who wore the necklace you've got on? Take it off; it reeks of her blood! Blood everywhere, everything here is stained with blood. I don't want any part of it! Take this back!" He tore off the sheathed dagger she had given him and threw it on the ground in front of her. "Have you ever seen a village after the raiders have gone? Have you—"

His voice broke. Turning, he ran blindly away, stumbling over the rough ground until he could no longer hear them calling after him.

It was Gordius who found him. Phaidon, lying facedown in the shade of some bushes, heard the small stones shift beneath the other boy's feet as he came toward him. He did not look up, hoping he was invisible in the deep shadow. But the footsteps stopped, and Gordius sat down beside him. Half opening his eyes, Phaidon could see his feet in their worn, much-repaired sandals. He shut his eyes again and did not speak.

"I told her about your parents," Gordius said. "She's crying. I never heard anyone cry so hard before. Her eyes are so swollen she can hardly see out of them. She's very fond of you, you know. You're her hero."

"I never wanted to be."

Gordius shrugged. "She was lonely. She had nobody, and you came along. You know, I feel sorry for her. You and I, we both had a mother and father when we were small, to care for us and tell us how to behave. What did she have? A bear and a pirate. It's a wonder she'd turned out as well as she has. She's brave. And look how generous she is."

"I don't want her generosity. She can keep the lot!"

"What about the captain's sugarplums you ate an hour ago? Are you going to throw them up at her feet?" Gordius asked, suddenly very angry. "She's never done you any harm. She taught you how to hunt. She's given you the best tidbits from her plate. She carried your spear for you when you were tired of tripping over it—and she's younger and smaller than you."

"I didn't ask her to!" Phaidon cried, flushing. "I didn't want her to fuss over me. I wish she wouldn't." He was extraordinarily hurt by the thought that the quiet boy, whose opinion he had never particularly valued, had all the time been silently watching and judging him. "All right, I'll say I'm sorry, if that's what you want. But I'm not taking anything of hers."

"It doesn't really belong to her, any of it. I think you're right," Gordius said. "The people it belonged to must be dead. But how can it harm them if we use it now to help us stay alive?"

Phaidon did not answer.

"If we take what we need, will you help us make the dummies," Gordius asked, "so that we have the chance to reach the mainland? Phaidon, will you? Not only for our sake, but for—" He broke off and did not complete his sentence, but Phaidon thought he knew what he'd been about to say: "For Cleo's sake, for your sister whom you seem to have forgotten, all these sunny days we've hunted and fished and run races over the sands."

"I haven't forgotten Cleo," he said, answering the imagined reproach. "I suppose you're wondering how I can laugh and make up comic songs——"

"No, I'm not," Gordius said, looking surprised. "I know you miss her. I've often heard you crying at night, even though you stuff your fists into your mouth so you won't wake us. Why shouldn't you laugh when you can? She'd have wanted you to. A priest once told me that grief is not a duty. You should let it come and go as it will and not bind it to you with iron hoops. Cleo told me that you had a happy nature. Don't lose it now."

Phaidon looked at him in astonishment, but somehow the other boy's words comforted him. When Gordius asked him again if he'd help with the dummies, he said yes.

They arrived back at the sandy bay late that afternoon and, having given all the food to Uncle Pelops, fended off his questions by saying they had work to do. He was too pleased with their gifts to argue. When, later, he came over to call them to their supper, he looked with what appeared to be genuine admiration at the dummy that was growing under Gordius's clever hands: at a torso made of ribs of curved green twigs, bound to a wooden spine by the stems of creepers; at the strips of cloth Phaidon was cutting that later would bind the frame like the wrappings of a mummy; at the mask Iris was making out of thin strips of bark and fish glue.

"Come and look, Dorian," he called. "Come and see what they are doing. I had no idea they were so clever."

CHAPTER 15

The quarrel was soon forgotten. For a day or two Phaidon went hunting alone, fished on the other side of the bay, and spoke to Iris only when he had to, in a carefully polite voice, while she, too proud to show that she was hurt, went off with Gordius or Dorian, smiling too brightly and not looking back. But every afternoon, when the hunting and fishing were done, and the day's food and wood gathered in, they came together to work on the dummies. And there, surrounded by the growing vegetable men, so ridiculous and ungainly with their floppy arms and hollow heads, they would suddenly find themselves laughing like friends once more, and it would be too late to draw back.

Six men they made out of wood and weeds and rags, one for each mouth of the monster. As they took shape, the fabricated crew began to acquire personalities and names. One, whose body turned out gross and squat, the neck short and brutal, Phaidon called Polydectes, after the old king of Seriphos.

"What was his face like?" Iris asked, sitting beside the dummy, with her box of colors on the ground beside her.

"Red and angry," Gordius said.

Phaidon shook his head. "Gray, when last I saw it," he told her. "Gray, with his mouth gaping open and his eyes bulging like onions. That's right," he cried, watching her as she mixed the powdered color with her fingers and smoothed it over the mask, drew in its eyes with a pointed stick dipped in black, bringing the terrified king back to monstrous life under her hands.

"Nobody would want to eat him," Uncle Pelops remarked. He and Dorian often came over to watch. "He looks poisonous—who's it meant to be?" he asked, suddenly suspicious. "Not me, I hope?"

She laughed and shook her head but agreed that she'd better make the dummy look more appetizing. Dipping her fingers into the jar of red powder, she mixed it quickly into the still-wet gray, producing a mottled crimson so like the old king in a rage that Gordius drew in his breath with remembered fear.

From then on she was careful to make the faces as tempting as possible, with cheeks flushed like ripe peaches or brown as new-baked bread. She gave them eyes like blue damsons or boiled sweets, and lips like berries. One turned out so beautiful that she named her Helen, after the lovely queen of Sparta and wanted to dress her in the women's clothes the captain had been bringing back for his wife, but they said it would look odd. You didn't find women among the oarsmen.

"I'm a woman," she said. "Very nearly."

"You don't look like one," Phaidon said, laughing, and she scowled at the dummy queen, as if suddenly envious.

When, weeks later, the figures were at last finished, they carried them down to the waiting boat, where their places had been already prepared for them. A wooden stake had been firmly bound to each of six benches, and a crossbar the width and height of a man's shoulders attached. To these the dummies were tied like prisoners, so that the rocking of the boat would not topple them. Then the pirates' cloaks were fastened around their necks to hide their bonds, and colored cloths tied around their heads, so that nothing showed except their faces and the dark tufts of hair glued into position beneath the headbands.

"Ye gods," Dorian said, stepping back to admire them, "you could take them for real men. Except no oarsman would wear a cloak when working. Let's hope that doesn't make the creature suspicious."

Uncle Pelops smiled in a superior way and said that the animal, whatever sort of beast it was, was unlikely to reason things out like a man. Animals couldn't take off their own skins when they were too hot, after all.

"Smell, that's what they go for. And these smell of wood and glue and—oof! Something rank and horrible. What is it! Decomposing weeds? That's what will give them away."

"We thought of that," Phaidon said. "Leave it to us. Just before we set out, we'll stuff their hollow heads with chopped fish and honey and wild mint. They'll smell so good we'll want to eat them ourselves."

"And when are we setting out on this journey?" Uncle Pelops asked.

"When the wind changes," he was told.

It was like waiting to have a tooth pulled. It gave them too much time to think about what lay ahead. Dorian kept frowning up at the clouds, always blowing the wrong way across the sky. Gordius was more silent than ever. Phaidon and Iris laughed too loudly, couldn't keep still, kept singing the monster song until Uncle Pelops screamed at them to shut up, shut up or he'd knock their noisy heads together until their teeth fell out.

"Only fools believe in monsters! How many times do I have to tell you, Phaidon, that there are no such things?"

"There are! I saw one! I saw the Gorgon's head—"

"Reflected in a silver plate, that's what you told me. Dear boy, it was probably the king's face you saw, distorted by a smear of grease left on the silver."

"It wasn't! I saw snakes growing out of her head like hair—"

"Smoke. Smoke from the torches. Look at the smoke from our fire, twisting and writhing. No, you imagined it all."

"You have to believe me," Phaidon said, hitting the ground with his fist. "You saw them! Cleo—and the king and all the stone lords. You saw them, too."

For a moment Uncle Pelops was silenced. Fear crept into his face, bulged in his eyes, trembled in his cheeks. Then he muttered, like someone repeating a creed, "There are no such things as monsters, no such things. . . . Disease, that's what it must have been, some terrible disease Lord Perseus brought back from foreign parts. . . ."

Before Phaidon could say any more, Dorian put his hand on his arm and frowned at him warningly. Later he took him aside and told him not to quarrel with his uncle.

"Why not, if he's wrong?" Phaidon demanded hotly.

"Because he took care of you when you were small and helpless. Now he's older and not as strong as he was. I expect his back aches and his knees are stiff and his feet hurt. He knows his days for fighting monsters are over. Can you blame him if he hopes he never meets one?"

"No. Of course I don't. But he says he doesn't believe in them."

Dorian shrugged. "All I know is he has nightmares every night and wakes me with his shouting. You, on the other hand, sleep soundly, snoring in your dreams like a bee after honey. You're not troubled by doubts. You know we are all in the hands of the gods. Pray to Poseidon tonight, Phaidon. Sing him your thank-you song again and perhaps he will send us a good wind."

Three days later, very early in the morning when the moon still hung in the sky like a misty pearl, the wind changed. It blew over the beach, setting the grains of sand dancing. It blew on the banked-up fire and woke its red embers to life. Flames leaped up through the covering of damp wood and weeds. Clouds of smoke rolled over the sleepers, who had thought themselves safe and now woke up choking and swearing and waving their hands angrily in front of their faces.

"What's happened?" Uncle Pelops demanded when he could speak, stumbling out of the smoke. "Who did that? Was it you, Phaidon?"

"No! I've only just woken up."

"It's the fire. Somebody must've poked it."

The others joined them, still half asleep, blinking their eyes and clearing their throats to grumble at the fire for changing its mind in the middle of the night. It was Dorian who said, "It's the wind. The wind is blowing the other way. The right way. We can go now."

Now? This very day? The sun would soon be up and the moon gone. They could already see one another's uneasy faces in the gray light of the coming dawn. The boat was ready, the dummies in place, everything packed except for the few things still in use. What was there to wait for?

"Might as well have breakfast now," Uncle Pelops said gloomily. "We can talk about it later."

"What is there to discuss?" Dorian asked. "We all agreed to go. You, too, Pelops. We're as ready as we'll ever be. Why sit biting our fingernails any longer?"

"Let's have breakfast and go," Phaidon cried, and won a smile of approval from Dorian. None of the others said anything, not even Iris. It seemed to him that she was avoiding his eyes. When they had breakfast, she sat between Uncle Pelops and Dorian and took no part in the argument they conducted over her head. This was so unlike her that Phaidon wondered if she was frightened. He got no chance to speak to her alone until Uncle Pelops sent them to wash the dishes in the sea.

"What's the matter?" he asked as they walked over the sands.

She would not tell him at first but said, every time he asked, "Nothing. I don't know what you mean. Nothing's the matter."

"Are you frightened?" he asked.

"I'm never frightened," she said untruthfully.

"I am. I'm frightened now. But I'd rather get it over and done with. It's the waiting that gets me down."

She appeared struck by this, because she nodded her head several times. They reached the edge of the sea and squatted down to wash the dishes in the cold water. "Dorian expects me to steer the boat," she said suddenly, as if she could contain it no longer.

"I know. None of the rest of us have ever done it. You have, haven't you?" he asked, suddenly doubtful. "You said you had."

"Yes, I have. I wasn't lying . . . I might have exaggerated a little. But my father did say I was good, well, quite good. Not bad at all for my age—and seeing I am a girl and the steering oar's so heavy. But he never let me take over anywhere near rocks. The captain forbade it. He said he'd have my head if I wrecked his boat. So I've only taken over in the open sea when it was calm."

"How often?" Phaidon asked, frowning.

"Four times."

That was four times more than the rest of them, he thought. She'd have to take them out of the bay. They needed the rest of them to do the rowing. . . . He couldn't bear the thought of staying, now that he'd screwed his courage up.

"Don't worry," he said. "You'll be all right. See how calm the sea is. I'll have to help row, but once we're out of the bay and the wind takes over, I'll come and help you. You can tell me what to do. We'll manage somehow. Don't let Uncle Pelops know, though, or we'll never persuade him onto the boat."

She smiled and said she wouldn't tell anyone else. She seemed so comforted by his words that now he began to worry. As they walked back with the clean dishes, he kept looking at her sideways, seeing how thin and small she was and wondering if she'd ever steered the big boat at all or whether it was all lies.

He had misjudged her. She might be small, but she was stronger than she looked, and it was obvious right away that she knew what to do. She looked quite at home, standing easily on the small stern deck, the long steering oar in her hands, her eyes alert for underwater rocks or hazardous currents.

They moved slowly and jerkily across the bay, an ill-matched quartet of oarsmen, he and Dorian on one side, Uncle Pelops and Gordius on the other, while in between them, the fabricated men swayed gently with the motion of the boat. Once they were out of the protection of the cliffs, the wind rushed at them, blowing their hair sideways and fluttering the ends of the headcloths on the dummies. Iris needed all her strength now to swing the boat around. Caught in the current at the edge of the whirlpool, it began to move more quickly. She shouted at them to ship oars and untie the sail, her voice sounding shrill and anxious.

Once under sail, there was no time to think. The boat leaped forward at such speed that the water rose on either side of the prow, and they seemed to fly forward on the wings of a great white bird.

Phaidon climbed up onto the stern deck beside Iris. His bare feet slipped on the wet wood, and he grabbed at the oar with one hand.

"What are you doing?" she shrieked above the wind.

"Can't I help?"

"Not like that. Put both your hands above mine—that's right. Only push and pull when I do. I'll tell you."

The steering oar jumped and shook in their hands. On their right, tall cliffs and jagged rocks rushed past, while on their left the whirlpool spun its glittering web to catch them. There was a terrible fascination about the wild water, rushing around in its ever-tightening coil until it toppled helplessly into the roaring mouth of the sea. Phaidon found his gaze drawn to it, and he forgot what he was doing till he heard Iris shout furiously: "Pull! Pull! Phaidon, help me!"

Hastily he tightened his grip on the oar and, with all his strength, helped turn the boat away from the deadly pull of the water. Now they were rushing between the edge of the whirlpool and the towering black crag, whose top was lost in clouds. Suddenly Dorian was beside them, shouting, "Hide! Hide! I'll take over now!"

Before they could argue, he picked them up and threw them down into the body of the boat. As Phaidon fell, he heard a shrill yelping somewhere above him and glimpsed a writhing tangle of what appeared to be monstrous snakes. When he'd landed with a painful thud between the benches, he looked up again and saw they had heads like dogs, not snakes, with thin reddish hair through which the skin showed in grayish patches, like mange. Their eyes were round, dull, and empty, their jaws long and snapping, overfull of slobbered teeth.

He saw one of the heads attack the sail, half ripping it from the mast before spitting it out in disgust. He saw Dorian standing on the deck, one hand on the steering oar, the other swinging the captain's ax around his head, warding off the two that were snapping at him. As he tried to get to his feet to help Dorian, one darted toward him, its jaws open and dripping. He dived beneath one of the benches on which a dummy sat and crouched there, hiding his face in terror.

There was a loud cracking and tearing sound, and he felt the trailing cloak of the dummy brush against his arm as it was whisked away. When he opened his eyes again, he saw the dummy had gone and there was nothing above him except the wooden bench and an empty sky.

He wriggled out from under the bench and looked around. The torn sail was loose and flapping over the benches. The dummies were all gone, and he could see no sign of Uncle Pelops or Gordius. Iris was crouching under the bench next to his, and on the stern deck he saw Dorian kneeling and clinging to the steering oar as if for life. His tunic was torn off his shoulder, and his arm was scarlet with blood. The boat, its sail practically useless now, was drifting on, carrying them out of the reach of the monster, whose six heads squealed with anger and disgust as they spat the dummies out into the sea.

"Uncle Pelops! Gordius!" Phaidon screamed, his eyes filling with tears.

There was an odd grunting noise, and the sail began flapping wildly. Phaidon blinked his tears away and stared as first Uncle Pelops and then Gordius crawled out from underneath, unhurt except for a bruise or two. They didn't know what had happened. Had lightning struck the mast? The monster? What monster? They hadn't seen anything at all.

"There!" Phaidon said, pointing, but a pale mist had risen out of the sea, and the six-headed monster, the black crag, and the whirlpool had vanished from sight.

III

PHAIDON

CHAPTER 16

Uncle Pelops had changed. Not only was he thinner, but he was quieter, and he sat for hours staring into space as the boat sped over the water under its mended sail. Sometimes his hands would move restlessly, patting his ragged clothes or feeling under the benches, as if still searching for his missing treasure. It was gone, the bag of silver and gold, swept over the side with the other bundles when the monster attacked, and must now be lying at the bottom of the sea. Nobody suggested going back for it.

Phaidon worried about him. He was fond of his uncle and almost wished to be shouted at again, anything to dispel the lost, bewildered look in his uncle's eyes.

It was left to him and Gordius and Iris to manage the boat, to mend the torn sail and repair the cracked yard. Dorian tried to help, but he was weak with pain and loss of blood. Iris had bathed his wounds in seawater, letting the blood flow freely to wash out any poison from the monster's bites. She then bound his arm neatly with strips of cloth and ordered him to remain in the bed they had made for him in the bottom of the boat, sheltered from the wind.

"You must do what you're told," she ordered, having lost her fear of him now that he was weak. "I know all about treating wounds. I often looked after the men. My father said I was better than any healer. He said I had the gift."

Dorian smiled at her gratefully, finding her boastfulness, which used to irritate him, oddly reassuring now that he had lost his great strength and was secretly terrified that he might lose his arm. He drank the bitter draft she gave him and slept, while the boat sailed on through a shrouded world.

The mist lasted for three days. Sometimes the sun shone through a hole in the clouds and they seemed to be sailing on a circle of gold through a white sky. At other times it swirled around them, confusing their tired eyes with its pale patterns so that they imagined sudden rocks and sea monsters where none existed. Several times they scraped the side of the boat against a crag they had seen too late. The stars were invisible at night, and they had no idea where the wind was blowing them. But fate was kind. The wind remained their friend, carrying them past dangers they never even saw, filling their crippled sail with a gentle and steady breath.

On the fourth day the mist cleared, and a bold yellow sun shone in the sky.

"Look!" Phaidon said, pointing.

"What? Where?"

"There! That long gray smudge. Is it a cloud or is it—"

"Land!" Gordius cried, and they all cheered, except for Uncle Pelops, whose eyes filled with tears, as if he couldn't believe it, as if it were too good to be true.

*   *   *

The following afternoon they landed in a wide sandy bay, leaving the boat in the shallows, almost too exhausted to lift the heavy stones of the anchors over the side before staggering up the beach to collapse in the nearest patch of shade. The last hour had been a confusion of terror and effort, with the boat rushing in too fast, and Iris, standing on the stern deck, the wind blowing her ragged tunic around her like a tattered sail, screaming out urgent and contradictory commands: "Lower the spar! Not so much! Look out! Ye gods, we nearly hit it. Use the oar. No, not that side!" Now that it was over, all they wanted to do was rest.

"I'm never going to sea again," Uncle Pelops said faintly, and closed his eyes.

The others lay back, content to let the rocking world steady and to enjoy the feel of the soft sand beneath their aching bodies and to drift into sleep.

Phaidon was the first to sit up, driven by restless curiosity. So this was the mainland, this wealth of woods and hills and sandy cliffs. He had never seen so much land before. From where he sat, the bay appeared to be encircled with mountains, layer upon layer of them, receding softly into the haze. He could no longer make out the opening through which they'd come. How could he ever find Cleo? The world was too big a place.

He got to his feet and, leaving the others resting, began to walk slowly around the bay. At first a small wood blocked his view. Peering through the trees, he had glimpses of a rough hill, the grass thick with weeds and rocks. Far away he heard a dog bark, but he could see no farmhouse or cattle. He walked on until the trees thinned out and were replaced by flowering yellow thistles as high as his knees. Beyond them he saw a road running along the top of a steep bank. On this road three people waited.

They were women, old women dressed in black. They sat

hunched on the backs of three patient mules. He knew they were waiting for someone; there was an air of expectancy about them.

One of the mules shook the flies off its ears. Another shifted its feet. The fat old lady craned her neck forward and peered down into the bay.

"He should be here by now," she said.

Then the tallest of the three caught sight of Phaidon. She murmured something to her companions, and they all turned around and looked at him and nodded their heads, as if he were the person they were expecting.

Before he could greet them, the tall one called out in a surprisingly powerful voice: "See you in Anaktaron!" Then they turned and rode away.

"Wait! Don't go! Please, can you help me!" he shouted, but they did not look back. He began running after them. The sharp thistles tore at his feet, and the bank was so steep. By the time he reached the road at the top, the three riders were out of sight.

Oddly disturbed, Phaidon returned to the beach and told the others about the old women.

"They must have mistaken you for someone else," Dorian suggested. "It is odd, though. Why wait for someone and ride away the moment they come?"

"Perhaps they only wanted to deliver their message," Gordius said.

"What message?"

" 'See you in Anaktaron.' Must be a farm or a village." Uncle Pelops sighed. "Pity you didn't ask the way. I hope it's not far."

They were hungry. They kept telling one another they were lucky to be alive, but they didn't feel lucky. They had lost almost everything, their food gone, their waterskin almost empty. They had had two cloaks among the five of them, and their clothes were in rags. All that was left of Iris's inheritance were her father's knife and the small leather pouch of trinkets that hung from her belt. All the rest was at the bottom of the sea. Dorian was the richest of them now, with his jeweled dagger and the gold buckle on his belt. "Which I'll gladly give to the first farmer who'll offer us food and decent clothes," he said.

"First we have to find the farm," Uncle Pelops pointed out gloomily.

They set out. Any farm or village would do, but having been given a name, it stuck in their heads. Anaktaron. As they made their way wearily up the steep, winding road, Phaidon encouraged himself by imagining a sunny kitchen, with jugs of milk and plates of bread and cheese on the table and a bowl of cool water on the floor in which to bathe his burning feet. But he could not fit the three old women into this pleasant scene. They intruded like dark shadows, watching and waiting, nodding their heads when they saw him as if he were the one they had expected. *But how could he be?*

It was a long, weary walk. Iris, walking beside him, kept stumbling on the stones. She must be even more tired than he was, he thought, and remembered how gallantly she had steered the boat, holding on to the long, heavy oar, peering through the mist with aching eyes, sleeping in snatches while he or Gordius took over. . . .

I must take care of her, he thought. *We owe her our lives. It's our turn to look after her now. I must see she doesn't get into any fights with the village boys. It won't do if she starts using her knife on them, and how else can she win? She's as free and wild as the bear who suckled her, but she's only young.*

It was a long, weary walk. The sun was sinking in a bloodred sky by the time they saw the farm ahead of them. They shuffled to a stop. It was bigger than they expected, a fine two-story building, surrounded by many outhouses. There were horses in the paddock at the side, and they could hear dogs barking furiously.

"They don't sound very friendly, do they?" Uncle Pelops remarked.

"They're only dogs," Dorian told him. "They'll do what their masters tell them."

"That's not my experience with dogs," Pelops said sharply, for there were times when Dorian's lordly airs got on his nerves. "And what makes you think that their masters will welcome us? We're hardly the sort of people I'd let into my house when night was falling."

They had to agree to this. They were a raggle-taggle lot, their hair unkempt, their faces gaunt and burned by the sun, their clothes in tatters.

"After what we've been through, they can hardly expect us to look our best," Dorian told him. "I'll go ahead myself, if you're afraid to."

"No, not you of all people," Pelops said quickly. "I don't think you realize, Dorian, just how villainous you look, with your tunic covered in old blood and your arm puckered up like raw beef, and your being so very big, you know. They'd set the dogs on you before you had a chance to open your mouth. No, we must be sensible. Let's sit down and think it out. It might be better to leave it till morning."

"Hadn't we better decide on a story to tell them?" Gordius asked. "We don't want them to guess we're runaway slaves. Who are we going to say we are? Farmers? Sailors? And what about you, Iris? Do you want them to know you're a girl?"

"No! Not yet. Not at first anyway. Call me Irus," she said, giving the masculine form of her name. She looked around to see if

Phaidon agreed. He had been sitting a little behind her, but he was no longer there. She could not see him anywhere. The others were arguing and had not noticed. Silently she slipped away to look for him.

CHAPTER 17

Phaidon was so hungry that he could not bear to wait for morning. Besides, what good would it do? They'd still be just as ragged and wild-looking, and farmers were always busy in the mornings. The sight of a tree, leaning conveniently against the wall that enclosed the farm, gave him an idea.

One of its branches hung low enough for him to catch hold of it and pull himself up onto the top of the wall, but unluckily the dogs heard him and came racing around the corner. The leader, huge and gray, more wolf than dog, leaped up and nearly caught his foot in its jaws. Frightened, he scrambled farther up the tree.

Once safely out of reach in its leaves, he laughed and wriggled his bare foot childishly above their noses, hooting like an owl when they jumped for it and missed.

"Phaidon?"

He looked down and saw Iris looking up at him.

"Go away," he said.

"What are you doing up there?"

He might as well tell her. "I was going to sing for our supper," he said. "I thought if they heard me singing, they'd be curious and come out, and then I could talk to them. They wouldn't feel threatened by a boy, and they might invite us in if I tell them we're harmless travelers."

"Funny they haven't come out to see why the dogs are barking," she said.

"They're probably used to it. Dogs often bark when it's getting dark and the wolves come down from the hills. No, don't come up! Wait there and see what happens; then you can run and tell the others."

To his surprise, she agreed meekly. "What are you going to sing?" she asked.

He hadn't decided. He looked around. From where he sat, high in the tree, he could see the distant glitter of the sea they had left, catching fire from the setting sun. Filled with a sudden joy at being alive and unharmed, he began to sing his thank-you song to Poseidon, and the three dogs below him threw back their heads and howled like wolves, either because they did not like his singing or because they wanted to join in.

They were so hopelessly out of tune that he started laughing helplessly, forgetting all his troubles. He did not notice the men who came around the corner until one of them called the dogs to him and told them to lie down, while the other, a gray-haired man, came and stood beneath the tree, looking up.

"Who's there? What are you doing? Come down!"

Phaidon slid from his branch until he was standing on the wall and could jump either way. "Please, sir, is this Anaktaron?" he asked.

The man stared at him. In the fading light Phaidon could see that he was handsome for his age, tall and thickset, dressed like a wealthy farmer. No knife at his belt, but a stout stick in one hand that could easily crack a head open. He was frowning.

"No, it's not," he said. "Anaktaron's half a day's ride away, and they don't welcome beggars there, any more than we do, so be off—"

"I'm not a beggar," Phaidon said quickly. "I'm a singer."

"I told you, Pa! I told you I heard singing," the other man cried, coming forward eagerly. He was young, with a round face and round eyes that stared as earnestly as a small child's. "It wasn't just the dogs howling, not but what they wasn't. I heard singing. Words. That's what I heard. Funny sort of bird we got in our tree, I thought."

"A bird, did you say?"

A third man, whom Phaidon had not noticed before, stepped out of the shadows. Though as tall as the others, he was thin, thin as a stalk, and dressed very finely, with gold glinting at his throat and on his wrists. His hair was sleek, and his face as pale as milk.

"Come down from there, and let me look at you, boy," he said. "Don't be afraid. The farmer and his son won't hurt you, will you, Nestor?"

"No, my lord," the farmer agreed, "and the dogs will not move unless Taras tells them to. My son is good with dogs," he added, and the young man smiled widely, his teeth showing white in the dusk.

"Come now, boy. I guarantee your safety," the lord said.

Phaidon sat down on the wall, careful not to glance behind him and give Iris away. Then he let himself drop down into the yard, landing with a thump that jarred all his bones and threw him forward onto his hands. When he straightened up, he found the three tall men looking down at him curiously.

"He's extremely dirty and ragged," the lord said, wrinkling his nose. "Not like any singer I've seen. Do you know him, Nestor?"

"No, my lord. He's not a local boy. He looks like a beggar to me."

"And yet your son heard him singing in your tree. Humor me, Nestor, I'd like to find out more about this strange bird. What's your name, boy?"

"Phaidon, my lord. And I'm sorry. I didn't know it was his tree. It grows outside the wall. I meant no harm."

"An innocent bird," the lord said in an odd voice, and the farmer turned to stare at him.

"My lord, you don't think *he* is—"

"I think he is a young scoundrel. I think he heard about the oracle and saw a chance to trick some wealth his way. Do you take us for fools, boy?"

"I don't know what you mean. What oracle?" Phaidon asked, bewildered.

"Sitting in a tree and singing like a bird! Asking if this farm is Anaktaron—where have you come from that you don't know Anaktaron is a great palace?"

"We only landed this morning," Phaidon cried. He felt nervous. The dogs were growling again, and the tall men looked threatening. He stammered out the story of their journey, but he was becoming dizzy with tiredness and hunger, and even to his own ears, it sounded an unlikely tale.

But at least they listened to him, asking an occasional question: Where had he come from? Kapnos? Where was that? He didn't know. How many of them had been in the boat?

"Five," he said, "there are only five of us. We are no threat to anyone. Only my uncle and Dorian are grown men, and we are all weak with hunger. We lost everything in the sea, all our food is gone. . . . When we saw your farm, we thought . . . we hoped . . ."

"Not a beggar, I thought you said," the farmer grunted.

"I'm a singer, sir. I can sing of love or war, or if you don't like songs, I could do your milking for you in the morning and you could lie on in bed."

He had been addressing the farmer, but all the time he was conscious that it was the other man who would decide what should be done with him.

"An extraordinary tale," the lord said. "What do you think, Nestor? Are we to believe him?"

"I couldn't say, my lord. I wouldn't have thought so myself, but still, I have heard tell of six-headed monsters . . . travelers' tales, you know what they are. . . . But what was he doing up in my tree?"

"That's what I keep wondering. Well, boy?"

"You can see the sea from up there," Phaidon said quickly. "I wanted to thank Poseidon for giving us a good wind. Poseidon is our sea god," he explained, uncertain if they worshiped the same gods on the mainland and wanting to show he had a powerful protector.

"It is the custom here to treat the gods with respect," the farmer said disapprovingly, "to bring them gifts of wine and meat, not come to them empty-handed and dressed in dirty rags."

"I promised him a song," Phaidon said. "He knows I have nothing else to offer. And knowing it, he helped me before."

To his surprise, they seemed impressed by this. The farmer and his son looked at him round-eyed, and the lord said, "So you are favored by the god, are you? He saved your life and blew you to our shores. . . . For what purpose? I wonder. Nester, I think we must hear him sing. Let's go inside."

"What about my uncle and the others?"

"Ah, yes. I'd forgotten about your family. Where are they?"

"Here!" Iris called.

They turned and saw what the dogs had seen some time ago and been shushed for growling at: Pelops, Dorian, Gordius, and Iris, sitting in a row on the wall.

"Ye gods, what clowns," the lord murmured, but Phaidon did not hear him.

His family, he thought, looking up at them. It was true, they were his family now, all of them. The dangers they had been through together had bound them closer than brothers. Poor Cleo was lost, and he would never rest till he had given her a proper burial, but at least fate had given him a new family to love.

The farmer's wife did not approve of them, even though they had washed their hands and faces and feet, but she fed them well. She listened to Iris's vivid account of their adventures with a small, tight smile of disbelief, but gradually her lips parted and her eyes grew round, and in the end she was listening as openmouthed as the youngest farmhand. By the time it was Phaidon's turn to perform, she was quite won over.

He sang his thank-you song to Poseidon, at Lord Telamon's request (for that was the pale lord's name). When he had finished, they were all silent for a moment.

Then Lord Telamon said, "You have a pretty voice. I don't wonder Poseidon has made a pet of you. It would be a pity to drown such a singer." He turned to the farmer. "Send the boy up to us tomorrow, Nestor. I'll leave my groom with the spare horse, and he can bring him up in the morning. I must return to Anaktaron tonight. I'm late already."

"What about the boy's family, my lord? Shall I send them with him?" the farmer asked.

"If you like, but they'll have to walk. I have no more horses to spare. If they're troublesome, we can always throw them down the ravine."

It was meant as a joke, but Phaidon did not laugh with the others. He was remembering three old women in black, nodding their heads at him as if he were the one they had been waiting for. "See you in Anaktaron."

CHAPTER 18

The horse was black and glossy. Phaidon could not believe it was meant for him. On Seriphos horses were for the nobility, not for slave boys. Donkeys were all he'd ever ridden, bareback and usually without permission. When the groom, Tiphys, told him to get up, he stared.

"Me? Don't you mean my uncle, sir?"

"Not unless your uncle is a boy called Phaidon who can sing like a lark."

Uncle Pelops came hurrying up. "What's this? The horse is for me, surely? I am Pelops, the boy's uncle. The head of the family." Seeing the groom was unimpressed, he added pathetically, "And I have bad feet."

"My lord said the boy was to ride," Tiphys grunted. "And the rest of you to walk. Those were my orders."

"But he can't have realized . . . too far for an old man to walk . . . the creature could carry us both . . ." Pelops babbled, but

the groom ignored him. Seeing how Phaidon still hesitated, he
lifted him up and tossed him onto the back of the horse, telling
him to hold on.

Phaidon grabbed the mane with both hands as the horse fid-
geted. Tiphys, now mounted on his own horse, jerked the leading
rein, and they moved out of the yard, with the walkers trailing
behind. The groom seemed to be in a bad mood. When Phaidon
asked him about Anaktaron, he shrugged and said: "You'll see it for
yourself—that is, if we ever get there at this snail's pace." It was
obvious he resented having to take them with him.

Phaidon felt both nervous and excited. Last night the farm people had said that Anaktaron was the palace of their king, who was a
great warrior. It didn't belong to Lord Telamon, as he'd supposed.

"You're lucky to be going there, a boy like you," the farmer's
wife had said. It was obvious that she still thought of them as
beggars, in spite of the lies they had told about having been wealthy
craftsmen, forced to take to the sea after their island had exploded.
Perhaps, even if she had believed them, no tale of past riches could
make up in her eyes for their present rags. "I can't think why they
want you there," she said, "unless it's to entertain the soldiers. The
king already has a minstrel. A proper one, trained by the best
teachers."

"My nephew is used to singing before kings. He sang for our
king back home," Pelops said, offended, but she sniffed, unimpressed by an unknown king on an island she'd never even heard of.
She said she doubted if Phaidon would even see the king at
Anaktaron, except in the distance. The palace was big, big as a small
town behind its high walls.

"Are there many statues?" Phaidon asked eagerly.

"Of course," she said, but when he asked her what they were like, she seemed unable to describe them with any other words than "big" or "the best."

Her eldest son, Taras, who was sitting next to Phaidon, leaned over and whispered in his ear, "No good asking her. She's been up there only once, and that uninvited. She come up in the cart when we was delivering some sheep. Never took her eyes off the fine lady's dresses. No good expecting her to notice statues. You interested in statues?"

Phaidon hesitated, but the young man's face was friendly, so he said, keeping his voice low, "The captain of a merchant ship stole a —a statue from us, the statue of a young girl holding a silver jug. I wondered if he'd already been here before us and sold it to your king."

The young man scratched his head and said he didn't remember seeing a statue like that, though that didn't mean it wasn't there. "Like Ma says, Anaktaron is big. I haven't seen more than the bit around the storerooms. I did try to have a look around at first, but the guards frowned me off. Must've thought I was a spy. Suspicious lot they are up there. If the king's got your statue, you'll have a hard job getting it back, I reckon. You could ask, though it's not something I'd care to do."

"Your mother doesn't think I'll get a chance to see him."

"Ma don't know everything," Taras said, with simple pleasure. "You'll get to see the king all right. Lord Telamon is set on it. I heard him talking about it when I brought his horse last night. Something to do with this oracle they keep talking about."

"What oracle?" Phaidon asked curiously, remembering the lord had said something about an oracle, but Taras shrugged and said he didn't rightly know. His father had told him, but he hadn't rightly understood.

"Anyway, I can't see the sense in consulting oracles, since all you ever get for an answer is a riddle, like as not. Best wait and see what comes up, instead of bothering the gods, that's what I say."

It was probably good advice, Phaidon thought, as he rode beside the silent groom. He couldn't resist turning to Tiphys, meaning to ask him if he knew. But before he could put the question, Tiphys set the horses into a gallop.

Phaidon, forgetting all about the oracle, clung on with hands and legs, sliding and bumping on the horse's broad back, feeling the wind in his hair and seeing the dust rise like smoke around the horse's legs. Once he slipped sideways and thought, *This is it!* But Tiphys, who was riding so close beside him that their knees often touched, reached out and yanked him upright again.

Phaidon laughed with excitement. "Good lad," Tiphys said approvingly. "So you're not just a pretty face after all. I could make a rider of you, a racer."

The gallop had put the groom in a good humor, and he stopped to let the others catch up. Seeing Pelops puffing and limping, he relented and let him ride in Phaidon's place, warning him that when they came in sight of Anaktaron, he'd have to change with the boy again.

"I'm not having the sentries tell my lord that I disobeyed his orders," he said.

It was nearly noon before coming out of a wood, they saw Anaktaron in the distance, circling the top of a low mountain like a pale crown, its stone walls yellow in the sunlight. A large plain, on which herds of horses were grazing, lay between them.

"We'll have a bit to eat in the shade of these trees," Tiphys said. "Then I must go ahead with the boy, and you can follow at your own pace. You can't get lost now. Follow this road across the plain, and it will take you right up to the main gate. I'll leave word with the guards to let you in. You should be there well before dark."

"I don't know how I'll manage it on my poor feet," Pelops complained. "Surely Lord Telamon wouldn't mind—"

"Orders are orders," the groom said curtly, and took the horses off to tie them to a convenient branch.

"Surly fellow," Pelops grumbled, looking after him. "I know the type. I've had them in my kitchen. Tell them to watch the stewpot, and that's all they'll do. Never mind if it boils dry; they'll just sit and watch it burn. Idiots."

Although he said this in a low voice, perhaps it wasn't low enough, for the groom remained in a bad temper while they ate their food, sitting a little apart from them until they'd finished eating. Then he ordered Phaidon to hurry up so roughly that the boy thought it better not to argue. He mounted his horse without protesting, only calling a quick good-bye to the others before they set off.

It was terribly hot on the plain. The sun was high in the sky, and there were no longer any trees to provide shade, only low bushes, tall thistles and dark red poppies scattered in the bleached grass like a hero's blood. The palace did not seem to come any nearer. Behind it the distant mountains had faded into a heat haze, and whichever way they looked, he could no longer see the sea.

It was too hot to gallop now. Phaidon kept looking back, but after a while he could no longer see the walkers on the long, white, dusty road.

"Don't worry," Tiphys told him kindly. He seemed to have recovered his temper. "They can't get lost. All they have to do is keep to the road, and they'll get there in the end."

It was a long walk, Phaidon thought. Uncle Pelops had looked so tired, and the others had been unnaturally quiet, as if they had no breath to spare for talking. But their eyes had been hopeful, and they'd talked of Anaktaron as if already counting on finding a place there, a home. "The king is sure to like you," Uncle Pelops had said, "and then we'll all be set up, dear boy."

Supposing the king didn't like him . . .

Phaidon put his hand up to his throat uneasily. His mouth was dry with the dust from the road; his throat burned. He felt he'd never be able to sing again.

The road began zigzagging steeply uphill, and they walked their horses for a while to rest them. Looking up, Phaidon saw the high walls of Anaktaron outlined against the sky and, a little farther down, the glint of armor in the sun as a sentry leaned out from some hidden shelter to take a look at them.

After they remounted, they passed a hunting party going the other way, with their spotted hounds yelping around them. Then two groups of soldiers in light armor marched by, their eyes moving sideways in their set faces as they passed.

"Is your king at war?" Phaidon asked.

"He wasn't when I left home yesterday," Tiphys said. "Though he had been recently and will soon be again, no doubt. He's that sort of man. But at the moment all is quiet—until you start to sing."

"I hope my singing won't start a war," Phaidon said, laughing.

"He doesn't fight boys. He has them whipped. So mind your manners, lad. Our king has a quick temper." Catching sight of Phaidon's gloomy face, he added kindly, "Cheer up, lad. It may never happen."

Phaidon smiled nervously. The nearer they came to Anaktaron, the more he wished he were somewhere else, but there was no going back. The road now ran between high walls, shutting them in, casting cold shadows. At last they came to a huge gate, clad, like the soldiers who guarded it, in beaten bronze.

Phaidon, trying not to look frightened as the gate clanged shut behind them, succeeded so well that he looked bored.

"You don't seem impressed," Tiphys complained as they rode up a wide paved way between fine houses, many painted and pillared, with benches on either side of their doors and dogs sleeping in the afternoon sun. "I know you're used to palaces, my little songbird, but be honest, was your king's palace half as fine as this?"

"No," admitted Phaidon, "but I didn't want you to think I was a bumpkin, so I tried to keep my mouth from gaping. I've never seen anything like this. It's so big I can't believe it's real. It looks like a palace for the gods—" He broke off and frankly stared as two young women walked across a courtyard, their long, curling hair bound up with silver bands, their thin dresses blowing in the wind.

"Those are not goddesses, lad," the groom said, laughing. "Far from it."

They dismounted and handed their horses to a young soldier, then went through a narrow opening into a smaller courtyard. This one was empty, but Phaidon could hear sounds coming through a window nearby, water splashing and something creaking, like a turning wheel. Tiphys knocked on the door, and a cracked voice called, "Come in!"

He had expected to be taken to Lord Telamon, but there were only three old women in the room. Old women often wore black; they might be anybody. The room was full of steam. He could not see clearly. Yet he thought he recognized them: three old women dressed in black, waiting. . . .

The fat one and the middle-sized one were pouring hot water into a large stone tub, and as he stared, the tall one came toward him. Though she was wrinkled, with a prominent nose and wispy gray hair, she moved easily, with the air of a great lady, and her voice was firm.

"Ah, it's you, Tiphys. Good," she said. "So this is the boy Lord Telamon told us about?"

"We've met before," Phaidon cried. "Wasn't it you yesterday on the road above the bay? You and——and the other two?"

"My sisters? It might have been. We did go out for a ride in the morning——or was that the day before? I'm afraid my memory is not what it was."

"You said you'd see me in Anaktaron. How did you know I'd be coming?"

She raised her ragged eyebrows and shrugged. "Where else could you go? You were on the road that leads here." Her black eyes seemed to swallow him and spit him out again with disgust. Turning to Tiphys, she said, "He looks as if he hasn't washed since the last rain did it for him."

Tiphys, who had taken a liking to Phaidon, stood up for him, saying, "It's dusty on the road, lady. He was as clean as a fish when we set out this morning. Good luck, lad." He patted Phaidon's shoulder and left the room.

Immediately the three old women advanced on Phaidon through the steam. They caught hold of his tunic and began taking it off, screeching with laughter when he struggled and the cloth ripped.

"Don't! Stop! That's my only tunic!" he cried.

"Never mind, my pretty," the fat one said. "You shall have another made of the finest linen, with blue and silver thread woven into the border. We have been asked to wash you in hot water, three lots it will take, by the look of you. Then we'll cut your talons and tame your curls and rub you over with perfumed oil till you smell as sweet as roses, and altogether make you fit for Lord Telamon's——"

"No, no, you've got it wrong again, Clotho," the tall one said. "This boy is the singer they want for the king, hoping he'll turn out to be the bird of the oracle. Poor lad, he looks more like a young crow to me."

Phaidon opened his mouth to ask her what she meant, but they picked him up and dumped him down in water so hot that all he could do was yell.

CHAPTER 19

The four walkers arrived at the gates of Anaktaron while it was still light. Uncle Pelops was limping badly, grumbling dismally with every painful step. The others walked wearily but without complaining. They stood meekly when the guards challenged them, and Dorian kept his hand well away from his dagger, for the soldiers were well armed and had a nervous look to them that he didn't like.

"We are the family of Phaidon, the boy singer," he said. "Did Lord Telamon's groom, Tiphys, leave word about us?"

The soldiers relaxed. One of them, who seemed to be in charge, asked for their names but more as a formality than because he doubted them. Then he waved them through, telling a young soldier to go with them. "And don't loiter on the way back. Deliver them to Tiphys— No, I don't know where you'll find him. Use your head, man."

The soldier led them between large buildings, two and three stories high, that cast long shadows in the light of the setting sun.

They came out into an open courtyard, surrounded by tall red pillars, like a clearing in a burning forest. In the center, a small fire glowed redly in a square stone hearth, giving out a gentle warmth that was welcome in the evening air.

There were several people there, some strolling idly, some standing in groups and chatting, all dressed very finely. Gold and silver glittered on their arms and in their hair. When they caught sight of the newcomers, they turned and stared.

The walkers, streaked with dust and sweat and conscious of every stain and rip in their clothing, shuffled their aching feet and wished the soldier would hurry, instead of standing looking as if he'd forgotten where he was going.

Some of the people were laughing at them now and whispering behind their hands. A pampered, perfumed boy, in a soft blue tunic, with gold at his wrists and silver sandals on his feet, turned around.

"You're here!" he cried joyously, running over to hug them each in turn. "Oh, I am so glad to see you! I thought you'd got lost. I was afraid I'd never see you again."

"Phaidon? Dear boy, is it really you?" Uncle Pelops asked, staring. "You're so gorgeous. I took you for a lord, at least."

"I'm waiting to be shown to the king. If he doesn't like the look of me, I expect we'll all be—"

Before he could finish, the tall old woman in black hurried up and, pulling him away from them by one ear, began dusting down his tunic with her free hand, saying angrily, "I thought I told you to keep out of mischief! Who are these dirty peasants? Oh, I suppose they're your family. Well, you can't see them now. Take these people away," she said to the soldier. "They're to have one of the guest rooms. Find Tiphys, he knows about it." She turned to Uncle Pelops and flapped her hands at him dismissively. "Go away. I've no time for you now."

Dorian and Iris flushed with anger, and even Gordius clenched his fists. But Uncle Pelops had been a slave too long for a little freedom to go to his head. He turned meekly and went with the soldier. After a moment the others followed.

"How could you speak to them like that?" Phaidon cried, stamping his feet with rage and shame. "We are guests here, and free men, not slaves." If this was not true, what was the point of all they'd been through? "I've a good mind to complain to the king."

This threat merely amused her. Whoever she was, she seemed very sure of herself. "Ho-ho! High-flying now, are we?" she said. "Fine feathers don't change a goose into an eagle, my boy. Take my advice, and keep your mouth shut before the king. Speak only when you're spoken to, and take care to be polite. The king has thrown better boys than you to the dogs. Here comes Lord Telamon."

The pale lord was advancing toward them, almost hurrying; that surprised Phaidon, who had thought him too grand to jump to anyone's bidding. He looked Phaidon up and down, put a hand on his head, and turned him slowly around, sniffed at him, and then nodded his approval.

"You've made a different boy of him, Atropos," he said to the old woman, as if this were high praise indeed. "I'll take him now."

Phaidon followed him along passages and up a wide flight of steps into another courtyard, more brightly decorated than the last. Here lamps had already been lit, their flames reflecting in the armor of the guards who stood on every side. Lord Telamon led him across to some soldiers standing before what Phaidon took to be a painted wall, showing a battle scene with men in fighting chariots. While Lord Telamon spoke in a low voice to the soldiers, Phaidon examined the painting critically, thinking he much preferred Iris's work. This was more elaborate, but all the men had funny-looking long noses and big ears, and the horses were unnaturally thin in the middle. Suddenly part of the painting moved inward; it was a door.

"Come on," Lord Telamon whispered, pulling his arm.

The floor of the room they entered was of a creamy marble, so highly polished that everything in the room was faintly reflected in it: the painted walls, the soldiers in their dress armor, the high carved throne, and the king himself.

Phaidon, not daring to raise his eyes from the floor, saw the king first upside down, as dim pools of purple and gold and gray on the pale marble.

"This is the boy singer, my lord," Lord Telamon said.

"Have you a name, boy?" the king asked.

"Phaidon, sir."

"Look at me when you speak to me. And address me as 'my lord.' "

Phaidon looked up and saw at once where the artist had got the funny long nose and big ears from. The king was a plain man. His eyebrows were black and heavy. His eyes were hot and fierce. A scar ran down one cheek to his chin, and he had big red ears and a long nose with a twisted tip. He looked in a bad temper. Perhaps he was always in a bad temper.

"Yes, my lord. Sorry, my lord."

"Don't overdo it. One 'my lord' to one breath is enough. Do you play the lyre?"

"Our minstrel was teaching me, but I hadn't finished my lessons before I left, my lord."

"Have you a lyre?"

"No, my lord."

The king clicked his fingers, and a man came quickly forward and knelt before the throne, holding up a fine lyre made from the shell of a tortoise.

"Well, take it, boy, take it. I don't want it. I'm not a minstrel," the king said impatiently. "That's right. Now play something."

Phaidon's hands trembled so much on the strings that the first notes came out in a tangle, and he expected to be dragged away and whipped. When this did not happen, he gained confidence and played to the end of the simple tune he had chosen with no further mistakes.

The king sat, tapping his fingers on the arms of his throne, though not in time to the music. The arms were carved at the ends into lions' heads; with any luck, he'd get his fingers bitten.

"All done?" the king asked when Phaidon finished. "Good. Well, what do you think, Melos?" he asked, turning to the man who had provided the lyre. "You're the expert. I've no ear for music. Can he play?"

The man he addressed, who was thin and elderly, pursed his lips like a lemon-eater and would, Phaidon thought, have condemned him to the dogs had not the king added, "Lord Telamon says he has a pretty voice."

Thus warned that the boy had some support, Melos said grudgingly: "He has a small talent, my lord, but he has been badly taught. Still, he's young. Given time, I might be able to make a passable musician of him."

"You can't have much time," the king said somberly. "Take him away with you, and see what you can do with him in a week. I want him ready for the queen's birthday."

"My lord," the old man protested, "I thought *I* was to play at the queen's feast. I always have done before—"

"This year you can have a rest. The boy is to sing. Now, don't cry, you stupid creature. You can play a tune or two, if my lady is not too tired to listen to you again. But I want the boy ready. And you, boy, work hard. If Melos tells me you've been wasting time, I'll have you whipped. Take him away now."

Melos had been the resident minstrel at the palace for as long as anyone could remember, and now to have this sudden rival thrust on him was almost more than he could bear. As they walked away from the royal quarters, he looked sideways at the boy, hating his pretty face and his bright eyes and the easy way he walked in his silver sandals, as if treading on air. No rheumatism in those young knees, no swelling knuckles to make plucking the strings of the lyre an agony. And he was supposed to train his supplanter—it was too cruel. If he taught the boy badly, as he was tempted to do, fixed the lyre so that the notes came out sour, the boy would be whipped, but he, too, would be blamed. If he taught the boy well—though what could one do in a week?—then what would happen to him? Who would want an old singer whose voice had grown thin and cracked and whose fingers could no longer coax beauty from a lyre?

"You can have your first lesson now," he said, hoping to make the boy miss his supper; he himself could do with little food. "There's only a week to try to turn a fumbling boy into a passable player. You'll have to work all day and half the night, do you understand?"

"Yes, sir," Phaidon said cheerfully. He who had outwitted a six-headed monster was not going to be afraid of this old windbag.

Melos took him to a room a long way away from the royal quarters, whose windows looked over the wall and across a ravine to the mountains on the other side. The moon was up, silvering some peaks and throwing others into deep shadow. Melos poked the fire into flame and lit a small lamp. Telling Phaidon to sit down on a stool, he asked him what songs he knew and chose one for him to sing, saying he would accompany him himself on his lyre.

That would be a good way to throw the boy off-balance: play a difficult, changing rhythm, trip the boy with unexpected notes, make a fool of him by altering the tempo, destroy his confidence, tie his tongue in knots. . . .

But when Phaidon began to sing, Melos knew he could not do it. Never had he heard a more lovely voice. Tears came into his old eyes. He knew he must teach the boy to the best of his ability, even if it led to his own dismissal. He loved music too much to try to damage something so beautiful. Even though it was a beauty that could not last, for how long would the boy have until his voice broke?

CHAPTER 20

The tall old woman, Atropos, interrupted their lesson, coming bustling in without knocking, carrying a bundle of clothes in her arms. She made Phaidon change his blue tunic for a plain one and his silver sandals for brown leather and stripped the thin gold bangles from his wrists, telling him finery was to be worn only when he was sent for by the king or his lady, not to dazzle the eyes of slaves.

"If you mean me, Atropos," the minstrel said, "I'm not a slave nor ever have been."

"Don't boast," the old woman said. "We are all slaves to something."

"Even the king?" Melos asked, hoping to catch her out.

"Especially the king," she told him. "He's bound by tradition and all sorts of foolish and antiquated ideas. Also, he is in love, poor fool."

"I shouldn't repeat that to anyone, Phaidon," Melos advised. "It may be safe for the lady Atropos to say such things, but you could land up with your head cut off, and strange as it may seem, I wouldn't want that."

"True," Atropos said, laughing. "He'd better run off to bed before he hears things unfit for his young ears. Here, take these," she said, thrusting a bundle into his arms. "They're for—I forget her name—the girl who's pretending to be a boy. Iris, that's it. I told her I'd send them back with you."

"Pretending to be a boy? Who's this, Phaidon? Your sister?"

"My sister's dead," Phaidon said, and turned away to hide the sudden tears that stung his eyes, only half hearing the instructions Atropos called after him—first left, down some steps, then right and right again, through a narrow arch. . . .

The crooked moon lit his way as he ran through narrow passages and across wide courts, losing all sense of direction, forgetting what he'd been told. He passed a pale temple from which the sound of chanting was coming, ran down endless steps—and straight into the arms of three guards, who stepped out of a dark doorway and caught hold of him.

"What have we here?" one of them demanded. He was a thickset man with short, tightly curled hair. "A boy, a running boy, a young thief, I'll be bound. What's this you're carrying, my slippery lad?"

He took the bundle roughly from Phaidon and unrolled it to reveal two girl's dresses, one yellow and one cream, and some long green and blue hair ribbons that fluttered in the night wind and would have blown away had not a second soldier caught them in his fingers.

"A bit young to be robbing girls of their clothes, aren't you, lad?" he said, and they all laughed loudly.

"Let's have a look at him," the third soldier said, and, grasping Phaidon by the hair, tilted his head back so that the light from the moon fell on his face.

"His cheeks are wet," the first soldier said. "He's been crying."

"Of course, he's been crying. He's been caught red-handed."

"He was crying before we caught him. I heard him sobbing as he ran."

"What's the matter?" the first one said, with rough sympathy. "Cheer up, lad. If you came by these things honestly, you've only to say so. What were you running from—come to that, where did you think you were going? There's nothing for you here. Nothing but the dead, and they don't want new dresses."

"The dead?"

"Look how pale he's gone," the second soldier said. "The Furies must be after him. What crime have you committed, boy, to be frightened of both the dead and the living, eh?"

"What dead?" Phaidon asked, trembling and confused.

" 'What dead?' he asks. The royal dead, lad. Whom did you think these grand tombs were for? Not for the likes of you and me, certainly. Didn't you know this is the place of the dead? Where did you think you were going?"

"I was looking for the guesthouse," Phaidon said, and the soldiers laughed, finding this very funny. He could smell wine on their breaths.

"Our king may be warlike, but he doesn't usually house his guests in tombs," one of them said. "Not right away, that is. Not till they've done something to annoy him. Is that it, lad? Have you trodden on the royal toe? In that case, you did well to run."

"I didn't do anything. It's not that. He wants me to sing for the queen's birthday."

They stopped laughing and stared at him.

"Are you the boy singer?" the first one asked.

"Yes. I'm Phaidon. The old lady—I forget her name—gave me these dresses for—for my cousin," he said.

The men looked at one another uneasily. "Sorry, lad," the short one said, "but how were we to know? We were only doing our duty. No offense, eh?"

"No."

"You won't go complaining of us to your master?"

"I haven't got a master. I'm not a slave," Phaidon said. For some reason, it was important for him now to be free. Like Uncle Pelops, he'd been happy enough as a slave on Seriphos. But Seriphos had been his home; this fortified palace was more like a prison. Everywhere you turned, there were armed guards and soldiers. It made him nervous.

The soldiers had been coming off duty when he'd run into them. Now they offered to see him safe to the guesthouse, so that he would not get lost again.

Iris was waiting for him outside, standing so still in the shadows that they did not see her until she stepped out. The soldiers, alarmed by the sudden movement, had quickly drawn their swords, but they laughed when they saw what they took to be a thin, fierce boy, his hand clasping a knife, confronting them with all the impertinence of a furious kitten.

"What are you doing with him?" she demanded. "Let him go! He's Lord Telamon's guest. The king himself sent for him. He's under the protection of a god. He's—"

"He's quite safe, young sir," the first soldier said, interrupting her before she could claim that Zeus himself would strike them down with his thunderbolts if they hurt one hair on Phaidon's head. "He got himself lost down by the tombs, so we offered to show him the way back. Isn't that right, lad? No harm done."

"No harm done," Phaidon echoed, smiling. They were friends now. Coming back through the place of the dead, they had asked

him for a song, to show there were no hard feelings. Not being one
to bear grudges, he'd sung them his monster song, teaching them
to join in the chorus. "Heads and necks, heads and necks!" they'd
roared happily, filling the night with their noisy music and the
scent of wine. They had not woken the dead in their tombs, but
only an angry sleeper, who came out of his door in his nightclothes
and shouted at them, threatening to report them to their officer.
They had all run off before he could get their names or memorize
their faces in the dark. Their laughing, scampering rush through
the night so warmed them to one another that they now parted like
old battle companions.

"Don't forget us, now, lad. We won't forget you. Anytime you
need a friend, you know where you can find us," they said as they
took their leave. "You can count on us, Phaidon."

"I wonder if I can," he said softly after they had disappeared into
the shadows.

"Who are they? Where have you been? What've you been doing?"
Iris demanded. "I've been worried. Your uncle said you'd be all
right, but he's so pleased with the guest room, he can't think of
anything else. Do you know we have a slave to bring us food and
water? And we're all to have new clothes."

"These are for you," Phaidon said, and thrust the dresses into
her hands. "An old lady sent them. I've forgotten her name. Octo—
Octopus or . . . something like that."

"Atropos. Was it you who told her I was a girl?"

"No. Not me."

Iris nodded. "That's what she said. She said she didn't need
telling, she could see for herself. I don't see how. I'm not fat, am
I?" she asked, squinting down at her chest. "I mean, I don't stick
out anywhere, do I?"

"No."

"How do you know? You didn't even look at me."

"It's too dark to see now. Anyway, you've always looked all right to me."

"Have I?" She sounded pleased, taking this as a compliment. "I didn't like that old woman, did you? Thalia—she's our slave—says everyone is a bit frightened of her and her sisters. She says the three of them only come occasionally and stay for a while. And every time they come, something happens."

"What sort of thing?"

"She says it's usually something bad. Like somebody dies. Or somebody is murdered. Or a sheep is born with two heads, or a tomcat has kittens."

"That's just superstition."

"Maybe. Do you know what else Thalia said? Only you mustn't tell. She says there's a rumor going around that this time they've come for a queen. They say the queen won't eat, and she's getting thinner and thinner, and when she's nothing but bones, the old women will pack her in their sack and carry her away. Then the king will go mad with grief and set fire to the palace, and we'll all burn."

"That's nonsense!" Phaidon said uneasily.

"You sound just like your uncle," she told him. "He says it's not surprising the queen won't eat; the food here is terrible. He says if he were the head cook, she'd soon be as plump as a pigeon. He's going to visit the kitchens tomorrow and give them a few tips. Dorian is going to help out in the forge, and Gordius has made friends with a clerk and is going to spend the day with him tomorrow, checking the stores. What do they do when they run out of fingers to count on?"

"Use their toes, I expect. We ought to be going in, Iris. They'll wonder what has happened to us."

"It's nice out here," she said. "Look at the stars. Besides, you haven't asked me what I'm going to do tomorrow, Phaidon. Don't you want to know?"

"All right. Tell me. What are you going to do tomorrow?"

"I'm going to help you."

"Me?" he asked, laughing. "You can't play the lyre, can you? You certainly can't sing in tune."

"I'm going to look for Cleo," she said, and, seeing him turn sharply toward her, added, "I'm sorry. When you were shouting at the ship, I only heard her name. I didn't know then that she was dead. Gordius told me what happened to her later. You don't mind my knowing, do you?"

"No."

"Gordius told me you vowed to give her a proper burial, a vow to the gods," she went on, her eyes round. Wild as she was, she respected the gods. "You've got to find her first, and I'm going to help you. I heard you asking that young farmer about statues. I've already looked in three of the courtyards and down by the storerooms, but there's nothing there. There's a big statue of Hera in the temple and several little ones made of gold. One of the women shouted at me. I think she was afraid I was going to steal one."

He was touched. She had done so much for him already. She was so foolishly brave he was afraid she'd get into trouble. Dorian had once accused him of being rash, but compared with Iris, he felt himself to be as cautious as his uncle. Cleo was dead. Nothing could hurt her now. It was the living who were vulnerable.

"Don't take any risks, Iris," he warned her. "I'm bound to have some free time. I can look. It's safer for me."

She looked disappointed, as if she thought he had not been grateful enough. "Can you get into the royal quarters?" she asked.

"No. Not unless they send for me. Nor can you. You'd never get past the guard."

"Won't I?" she asked, smiling. "Don't be too sure. I told Thalia my father was a sculptor. I said he'd done all the statues for the palace on Kekapnos and traded many others with the captains of merchant ships, so there might well be some of his here. She said most of the statues were in the royal quarters, and when I said I wished I could see them, she offered to try to smuggle me in with the slaves who work there."

"It's too dangerous. If they find out, they'll kill you both. The king's got a terrible temper, and the soldiers told me he's terrified of being assassinated; that's why he has so many guards. Don't do it, Iris. I forbid you to."

But she only laughed and said that he was neither her father nor her master, and she would do what she liked.

CHAPTER 21

The next morning Phaidon got up early and crept out of the guest room, stepping over Dorian, who was lying in front of the door. The air outside was sweet and cold, as refreshing as water on his skin, after the stuffy night.

The small courtyard was empty. A rolled blanket and sheepskin under the bench against the wall of the house suggested that the slave might have slept there, but there was no sign of her.

He sat down on the bench and, while he waited, practiced clicking his fingers, as people used to do for him, when he was a slave and they wanted him to come. He thought he would enjoy being a master for a change. Then a girl came around the corner, carrying a large jug. He thought she was Cleo.

They both stared at each other, equally startled. Then he saw she was younger and plumper than Cleo, her cheeks fatter and redder, and her round brown eyes as moist and yearning as a timid dog's.

Her simple dress was made of the coarsely woven, undyed cloth that slaves wore, that he had worn on Seriphos.

"Are you Thalia?" he asked.

"Yes, master."

"Don't call me that. My name's Phaidon. Phaidon, the singer."

Her eyes grew wider and rounder, but she didn't say anything.

"I want to speak to you for a moment. Come and sit down beside me. What's the matter? Of course, you can sit with me. Oh, well, stand if you'd rather, and I'll stand, too," he said, getting to his feet. "But at least put your jug down. It looks heavy."

She put it down on the bench. It wasn't a silver jug but one made of bronze, he noticed. When he had first seen her, he could have sworn it was silver. It must have been the light.

"It's about my cousin Iris," he said, and saw her bite her lip nervously. "She told me you'd agreed to try to get her into the royal quarters—"

"She promised she wouldn't tell!" the girl burst out. "She promised she wouldn't!"

"And she won't," Phaidon assured her. "Telling me doesn't count. I'm her cousin. We're as close as teeth and tongue. Her word is my word also. Neither of us will tell, so don't worry."

She still looked frightened, so he went on gently. "It was kind of you to offer to help her. I know you meant well. But it's too dangerous. If you were caught, you'd both be in serious trouble. At the very least, you'd be whipped and turned out of the palace to starve."

"I wouldn't starve, sir, my lord," she said, uncertain what to call him if he didn't want to be called master. "There's plenty of work in the fields at this time of year. And I'm good at it. I used to be a farm girl until the raiders came and took me to sell as a slave."

She said it so quietly, as if it were nothing out of the ordinary. Her eyes were dark and blank. What was she seeing? Had they burned her village, too? He was too moved to speak. He put his arms around her in silent sympathy, but she leaped away and, picking up the water jug, held it between them, as if to stop any further advances on his part. She was *stupid!*

"I was only trying to comfort you, not kiss you," he said angrily. "The raiders came to my village also." He drew in a deep breath, trying to be patient, and then said, "I don't want my cousin to be whipped and turned out of the palace, even if you don't mind, do you understand?"

"Yes, master."

"I know it's not easy to refuse her anything, but it's for her own sake. I'm older than she is. I have to look after her. You needn't refuse her outright, just say it's taking more time to arrange than you thought. Say the royal house slaves want to wait until after the queen's birthday feast, when there'll be fewer guards. Will you do this for me? Please?"

"Yes, master."

But she still looked sulky. He had not won her over. What could he offer her? He still owned nothing, not even the clothes he wore.

"If you do," he said, with his sweetest smile, "I'll make you a song in praise of your beautiful brown eyes. Would you like that?"

She smiled and blushed a little. "Yes, master."

He went off to his music lesson, feeling pleased with himself. He had forgotten that Iris had more to offer than a smile and a song. She was a girl of property, who still had some of the pirates' wealth, a bag of trinkets, among which there were bronze and silver rings, and necklaces of blue glass and amethyst and pink coral.

* * *

He was afraid that Iris would guess that he'd got at Thalia. Thalia, he thought, was too stupid to keep secrets. When he came back that evening, he was prepared for Iris to fly at him in fury. He was not prepared for a smiling young girl in a yellow dress, with a wide green ribbon in her dark curls and a thin silver bangle on her wrist.

He did not recognize her at first. It was only when she came mincing up to him in an absurd mimicry of a woman's walk and he saw the laughter in her eyes that he realized it was Iris, his wild companion, now transformed into this milk-and-water miss. Oddly, he felt a pang of loss for the fierce boy-girl who had shared their adventures with such courage and had told such amazing tales about herself. This Iris might be prettier and cleaner and smell as sweet as a flower, but nobody would believe she had been brought up by a she-bear. . . . Then he noticed the small scars still visible on her thin brown arms, the playful bite marks, or so she'd claimed, of her brother cub, and again he wondered.

"I've looked almost everywhere," she told him. "In all the court-yards, except the ones in the royal apartments. I went down as far as the barracks, and the soldiers whistled at me. Do you think I look pretty in my new dress, Phaidon?"

"You look all right. Did you see any statues?"

"No. Do you think I'm as pretty as Thalia?"

"No," he said honestly. She was too thin. Her elbows were sharp as thorns. He rather liked her face, though. "You don't look as stupid as she does."

"Thalia's not stupid," she said, and smiled. Then she asked him how his lessons had gone. They talked cheerfully about things they had done and people they had met. She'd seen Atropos, she told him, and the old lady had promised her she could have a short hunting tunic, like the ones the goddess Artemis and her followers wore. "I hate having these silly long skirts flapping about my legs all the time," she said. "I don't know how the women manage to work in them."

She seemed to have forgotten all about getting into the royal apartments to look for Cleo. He was glad. She'd only have got into trouble.

The next morning when he got up, he found Iris was gone. Her bedroll was stored neatly under a bench in the guest room, but there was no sign of her. She wasn't down in the courtyard. She wasn't down by the well. She didn't come in for breakfast. And Thalia, serving them with hot bread and fruit, never once met his eyes but kept her chin lowered.

She'll have a double chin soon, and serve her right, Phaidon thought furiously. He knew she'd betrayed him.

The others could not understand why he was worried about Iris.

"She's probably gone off somewhere on her own concerns," Uncle Pelops said cheerfully. "You know what's she's like. Wild as a cat. Badly brought up, poor girl." He'd obviously forgotten that he'd claimed to be her father. "Don't worry. She can look after herself, I'll say that for her."

Phaidon did not answer. When Thalia left the room, he followed her, and though she ran like a terrified mouse, he soon caught her.

"What have you done with her?" he demanded.

"I don't know what you mean, master."

"Oh, yes, you do. She's gone off into the—"

"Not so loud, master," she said, looking around nervously. "I couldn't stop her. How could I? I'm only a slave. And she had a knife hidden in her dress. She said she'd cut my throat if I didn't do what she said."

That sounded like Iris all right. He couldn't think what to do. If he went storming off to the royal quarters, he might precipitate the very trouble he feared. He could have shaken Thalia, but it wasn't really her fault. How could this soft mouse stand up to a girl suckled by a she-bear?

"She'll be all right, master," Thalia said. "There's forty slaves go in each morning to polish the marble floors, and when some are sick, others stand in for them. The guards just count them as they go in. The head slave vouches for them, and she's fixed."

"Fixed?"

"Bribed, master," Thalia said, lowering her eyes. "She'd vouch for an ape, that one, for a string of blue beads."

"Oh."

"Don't worry, master. The young lady will be all right."

But he couldn't help worrying. He went off to his lessons and made so many mistakes that Melos shouted at him and asked him if he wanted to get them both thrown over the wall.

"You'd better take the afternoon off," he said. "Rest. Take some exercise. Sit in the sun and think what will happen to us both if you displease the queen. Too many fools are counting on you to work a miracle. I try to tell them you're only a boy with a pretty voice, but it's no good. They all talk as if you're the answer to a prayer. You're the promised singer who's going to charm their queen away from death. May the gods help us, boy, if you fail."

"You mean the oracle, don't you? People keep talking—hinting. Do you know what it says, Melos? Do tell me."

But Melos shrugged and said it was all nonsense.

When Phaidon got back to the guesthouse, he saw Iris and Thalia sitting on the bench outside—no nonsense this time, he noticed, about the slave not sitting down with her superiors. They were talking and laughing together like old friends and did not notice him until he was nearly upon them. Then Thalia saw him, gave a frightened squeal, and ran away.

Iris smiled up at him, her face glowing with triumph.

"I did it," she said. "I got in and out again, and no trouble. I saw the king. I polished the royal floors. . . . You should've seen us, Phaidon. Twenty girls washing and twenty girls polishing. Marble has to be polished while it's still wet or it leaves smears. It was like a dance. The washers move backward, and the moppers advance, and behind them the floor shines, and you can see the colors of the ceiling in it, only pale, like in a shining mist."

"I know. I've seen it. That's how I saw the king first, in dim splotches, upside down."

"The best way to see him," she muttered. "He walked through with dirty feet and never a word of apology. The queen was too ill to get up, they said, so I couldn't get in to see her room. Only her personal slaves are allowed to clean it. But I spoke to one of them later, and she said there were only three statues in there. One was of a giant cat, one a man with the head of a bird, and one a man with the head of a dog. The queen is an Egyptian princess and worships strange gods, she said. She thinks she's homesick, and that's all that ails her. But others whispered to me that Zeus is angry with her for bringing her foreign gods into Anaktaron. However, my friend Perse says she is simply sulking because her father married her to an ugly old king whom she cannot love—"

She stopped for breath. She had been talking very rapidly and twisting her fingers. He thought she was nervous and chattered to hide what she didn't want to tell him.

"Cleo wasn't there, was she?" he asked.

"No. I'm sorry, Phaidon. I looked everywhere, in every corner, in every room except the queen's. But there's nothing that could be her, only huge statues of Hera and Zeus, and Poseidon with his little fishes. No girl holding a silver jug. No girl at all, only the slaves and me. I'm sorry, Phaidon. I don't think this can be the right palace."

"Oh, well," he said, trying to smile, "I'll have to go on looking."

"They're all so happy here," she said, after a pause, "Uncle Pelops and Dorian. I don't know about Gordius, he's always so quiet. Uncle Pelops said the head cook here welcomed him with open arms, practically begged him for any help he could give. Head cooks are free men here, not slaves. And Dorian has been offered a craftsman's job in the smithy. They're short of workers here, it seems. If you go, and the queen dies, they couldn't stay here. They'd have to come, too. People would blame us all for her death. Oh, they talk as if you were sent here by the gods to save her. The king went to consult the oracle at Delphi; it's all to do with that. I couldn't understand the prophecy—you know what oracles are like, they're never clear. It didn't mention you by name or say anything about a boy singer."

"What did it say?" he asked curiously.

She told him:

Death unrebutted will capture a fair queen, craving the lady.
Pray for the innocent bird to deny Death, saving our lady.

He stared at her in astonishment. "What's that supposed to mean? It doesn't make sense. And what's it got to do with me? I'm not a bird. Where are my feathers? Where's my beak? Why pick on me? They're stupid."

She laughed at his indignation. "You have only yourself to

blame. There they all were, watching out, waiting and praying for the bird of the oracle, and what do they find? You, singing in a tree. You must admit it was a little odd."

"What am I going to do?" he asked.

CHAPTER 22

There was nothing he could do but go on with his lessons, practice on the lyre, and learn new songs. On the day of the birthday feast Melos sent him away, telling him to go and walk in the fresh air and keep healthy.

So Phaidon wandered down to the gates and stood watching the people go in and out: the farmers with their laden carts, the young men with their hawks and horses, the beggar being turned away. The guards kept glancing at him and talking together. He was used to being stared at now. Everyone seemed to know him. People he passed called out greetings and wished him luck.

After a moment a young captain came over to him and asked if there was anything he wanted.

"I'm just looking."

"You're Phaidon, the boy singer, aren't you?" the man asked. "Do me a favor, lad. Go and look somewhere else. You're making my men nervous. We have orders not to let you out."

"Why not?" Phaidon demanded indignantly. "I'm not a prisoner. I'm a guest."

"Don't blame me, lad. I just follow orders."

"But—"

"I expect it's for your own safety. You're important to us, you know. Good luck tonight."

"Thank you," Phaidon said, and turned away.

There was no point in arguing. Even if the captain had flung wide the gates and told the guards to turn their backs, he couldn't have gone and left his family to take the blame. Iris was right. Uncle Pelops was happy here. Even in this short time his face had plumped out again with smiling, and his clothes smelled delicately of honey and spices. Dorian, too, was happy learning his craft and had made many friends in the smithy and stables. They all were welcome here. The fever that had made an invalid of the young queen had brought death to many in the palace, and the king's frequent wars had killed many more. They were short of craftsmen and good workers.

"The gods must have brought us here," his uncle had said, beaming. "Now I needn't dread winter any longer. It would've killed me, sleeping out in the cold with my old bones. Thanks to you, Phaidon, we've found a home here."

"Supposing the queen dies?" Phaidon asked.

"She won't, dear boy, she can't. It says in the oracle—"

"The oracle!" Phaidon said bitterly, and turned away.

There were too many people counting on him. He'd never felt so uncertain, so fearful before singing. They wanted more than just a singer, that was the trouble. They wanted too much. How could he save their queen? He wasn't a physician or a priest. And he wasn't the bird of their stupid oracle either!

As he walked across a courtyard, people crowded around him,

wishing him success, reaching forward to touch him as if he were a sort of amulet to bring them good luck. One woman thrust a little lame girl in his way. "Make her well, master," she pleaded.

"I—I can't," he stammered, shocked. "I'm only a boy. I can't cure anyone."

Iris came pushing through the crowd to his side. "Leave him alone," she said angrily. "He needs to be by himself. Go away!"

Phaidon was afraid they'd resent this, but immediately they apologized and began moving off.

"Thank you for your good wishes!" he called after them.

"Let's go up there," Iris said, pointing toward the outer wall. "There are steps leading up to a high walk, and we can sit in the sun. They won't follow us up there."

The steps were steep and slippery, polished by the feet of countless sentries going up and down, but the walk was wider than it looked from down below. A soldier was standing with his back to them, gazing out over the wall. He turned quickly when he heard them behind him but smiled when he saw who they were.

"Good luck for tonight," he said.

"Thank you."

"Is it getting on your nerves?" Iris asked. "Everyone wishing you luck, patting you as if you were a favorite dog? You look tired. Let's sit down here. There's another sentry farther on, but they'll leave us alone. I told them you'd want to be quiet. Look down there. Careful! Don't fall! See, that's the courtyard you were in. I saw them all gathering around you like wasps around honey and thought you might need help. I ran all the way down the steps. I could've broken my neck."

"I'm glad you didn't," he told her, smiling.

"Of course, you might have been enjoying all the flattery, but I didn't think you were. You looked nervous. I like it up here, don't you? It's peaceful. Look through that opening in the wall, doesn't the mountain look close? You feel you could almost touch it with your hand, but don't try. There's a ravine in between, where they throw people they don't like. Not from here, there's a special place up there, somewhere," she said, waving her arm vaguely. "They say you can see the bones down there in winter, when all the leaves are gone."

"Don't frighten me. I'm frightened enough already. I can't save their queen—"

"But it's in the oracle! The oracle says you will."

He was suddenly angry. "Where? Does it mention me by name? Does it say Phaidon from Seriphos will save her? Does it?"

She shrugged. "Oracles are like riddles. A bird could mean a singer," she said. "Some people believe the pattern of our lives is laid down by the Fates before we're born. Perhaps you were born to save their queen."

"No, I wasn't!" he said, hating the thought. It seemed to make nonsense of all he'd ever done. "Remember what a struggle we had getting here, remember how our backs ached and our blisters and how nearly we were wrecked? Are you telling me now that we could've sat back and we'd have landed up here without having to raise a finger? Is that what you think?"

"I only said some people believed it. Not that I did."

He sighed and glanced down into the courtyard, where people were gathering again. "*They* believe it, don't they? They're so certain I can cure their queen. They'll turn against me if I fail. They'll throw me into the ravine, if they don't tear me to pieces first." He smiled when he said this, pretending that he was joking, but fear lay like a stone in his chest.

Iris hesitated. Then, after checking that the sentries were too far away to hear, she muttered, "Her maids say she recovered from her illness some time ago, didn't I tell you? They say she could easily go out if she wanted to, but she prefers to stay in her room, pretending to be sick."

"Why?" Phaidon asked, astonished.

"To annoy the king. So they say."

"She must be mad!"

Iris shrugged. "Don't you ever want to annoy people?"

"No, I don't think so. I often do annoy them, but not on purpose. . . ." He remembered the king's savage dark eyes and frowning brows and wondered that anyone should risk upsetting such a violent-looking man. Still, it wasn't his worry. "So much for the oracle!" he said, laughing with relief. "Death will capture a fair queen, indeed! She won't die. She isn't even ill!"

Iris smiled, but he thought she looked uneasy. "What's the matter?" he asked.

"Nothing," she said. She wasn't going to tell him what else the maids had whispered: that the king had a murderous temper, and there was more than one way to die, even for a queen.

That night the queen was late for her birthday feast. The great courtyard was crowded with people, the tables laid and a couch prepared for her beside the king's great chair. The king himself stood at the foot of the steps leading to the royal apartments, talking to a visiting lord. Phaidon, standing a little way off with Melos, saw the king continually glance over his shoulder and his face darken as time passed and the queen did not come.

Then a woman ran down the steps and knelt at the king's feet, her fingers resting lightly on the ground like a sprinter's, as if ready to race away to escape his anger. People stopped shuffling and whispering and stood in silence to hear what she said.

"My mistress is not well tonight. She sends her apologies and asks that you go on with the feast without her."

"I'll come to her," the king said.

"She begs that you will not disturb her, my lord," the woman said quickly, getting to her feet. "She has taken a sleeping draft and does not want company."

Phaidon thought the king was going to hit the woman. He stood with his large fists clenched, fighting to control his anger. There was no sympathy in his face for a sick queen who was missing her own birthday celebrations. Perhaps he, too, had heard it whispered that she was only pretending.

"Go back and tell your mistress that I will see to it myself that she has the peace she craves," he said in a terrible voice. "Forever."

Silence. The people, gray-faced and openmouthed, stood motionless, staring at their king, hardly daring to breathe in case they attracted his attention. Then the woman fled up the steps, glad to escape. The king turned back. His bloodshot eye caught sight of Phaidon, standing in all his court finery, the pretty lyre in his hands, the silver sandals on his feet, and his pent-up anger burst out.

"Curse you and curse all oracles!" he shouted. "Get out! Get out of here before I kill you! You're not wanted any longer, you chick, you peacock! Get away from me."

Phaidon ran. The crowd let him through, drawing away from him as if afraid his ill luck would contaminate them. He could not see Iris and the others anywhere and hoped they'd have the sense to hide. He'd nearly reached the nearest way out when the king sent a great shout after him: "Guards! Take that boy!"

He tried to run faster, but the doorway, which had been empty, was now filled with bronze breastplates and reaching hands. He stopped. Somebody behind him crowed with triumph and pushed him into the arms of the guards. Rough hands grabbed him and lifted him off his feet. As he was carried off, he heard the king's angry shouting in his ears: "Get rid of him for me!"

CHAPTER 23

One of the guards carried him over his shoulder like a sack of grain, so that his head hung down at the back. All he could see was the man's legs, thick and hairy in the moonlight. He heard the clatter of other feet behind him on the stairs.

The men were arguing among themselves about what the king had meant.

"It seems hard to kill him," one said. "He's only a boy. What's he supposed to have done?"

"It's not for us to question the king's orders—"

"Not even when the orders are unclear, like now? 'Get rid of the boy' might mean throw him into the ravine, true enough. Or cut his throat. Or push the poor little beggar out of the gates. I vote we do the last."

"And I say the ravine. I saw the king's face. Murderous, it was. Mad as fire. I don't want to have to tell him we didn't have the stomach to obey him."

The guard who was carrying Phaidon put him down abruptly, keeping a huge hand on his shoulder. "Make up your minds," he said to the others. "He's heavy, and he wriggles like an eel. I'm not carrying him farther than I have to. Which is it to be, the ravine or the gates?"

"The gates!" Phaidon begged, but the man cuffed him and told him to shut up.

"You keep out of it. It's none of your business," he said, seeming to forget it was Phaidon's life they were discussing.

Phaidon's ears rang. He felt sick and dizzy just when he needed to have his wits about him. It was unfair! He didn't want to die just because he'd got in the way of the king's anger.

He looked around. They were on a flight of steps between the outer wall and the royal apartments. In the shadowed building, three lighted windows shone like dim echoes of the pale moon. Ahead he could see the steps leading up to the top of the wall, and he thought with terror of the long drop down into the ravine, of the white bones that were visible in winter and the bears coming down the mountainside.

The hand that held him so firmly looked as tough as leather. Would his teeth even puncture it if he tried to bite it? Besides, where could he run to?

"You're making the wrong choice, Sergeant," the first guard was saying now. "Supposing the king changes his mind? There's no bringing the boy back once he's dead. Why don't we just lock him up until we see which way the wind blows?" Phaidon recognized him, though the other two guards were strangers to him.

"You're Nikos, aren't you?" he cried eagerly. "We met one night down by the tombs, remember? You had two friends with you, and we all sang together. You said I could count on you—"

"I remember, lad," Nikos said, looking embarrassed, "and I've been doing my best, as you could tell if you'd been listening. But I'm not in charge here."

"No, you're not. I am," the sergeant said irritably, "and I'm not taking any chances. Prisoners have a habit of escaping, especially when they have friends among the guards. No more talk, Nikos. Let's get it over with."

"No!" Phaidon shouted, struggling and kicking as they tried to drag him up the steps. The sergeant hit him so hard that he could taste blood.

"Try to be brave, lad," Nikos advised him. "Where's your pride? We all have to die sooner or later."

"Later! Later!" he yelled. Bruised and hurting from the sergeant's blows, Phaidon still clung to life. These might be his last moments, but he treasured every one: the feel of the cold night air on his cheeks, the scent of wet leaves on the dark mountainside, even the pain. . . .

He refused to go quietly to his death, just to make it easier for the guards. There was so much he hadn't done. He hadn't said good-bye to his friends. He hadn't buried his sister. She'd be lost forever between the living and the dead. "Let me go!" he screamed. "Don't kill me yet! I'm not ready! Somebody stop them!"

He was making so much noise that neither he nor the guards heard the women shouting down from the lighted windows, and it was not until a woman came hurrying around the corner that they realized they'd been overheard.

"Stop! You stop now," she said in a foreign accent so thick that it was difficult to understand. She was a short, stout woman, not young, though her hair was still black and glossy. "I take boy. My mistress want him."

The sergeant sniffed at this. His orders were from the king, he said, and took precedence over all others, even the queen's. They began arguing in the moonlight, while Phaidon looked again at the hand that held him and wondered whether to bite it and try to make his escape.

When Phaidon had been carried out of the great courtyard, his friends had tried to come to him, but there were too many people crowding between them, people who turned on them angrily, saying, "Who do you think you're pushing? Want a fight, do you?"

Iris was smaller and thinner than the others. She had sharper elbows and did not hesitate to use them. Besides, there was one advantage in being a girl. She found people gave way to her more readily. By the time she reached the doorway through which the guards had taken Phaidon, she had left Dorian and Gordius far behind.

Yet still she was too late to see which way the guards had gone. As she hesitated, she heard the sound of screams, shrill, angry, despairing.

She began to run. Her heart thudded. She tried to call to Phaidon but had no breath to spare. She ran and ran, hearing nothing but the sound of her sandals slapping against the paving and the thunder of her blood in her ears.

She was stumbling up steps now, her long skirts tangling with her legs. She stopped and kilted them up over her belt, then ran on. The dim moon, fretted by thin clouds, gave an uncertain light. On her left three windows glowed faintly in a dark building, but the steps curved to the right, became steep and narrow, climbing up toward the shadows near the top of the wall.

She stopped. Which way? She listened. She thought she could hear distant footsteps but could see no one. Behind her, men's voices shouted something. Then, from the top of the wall, she thought she heard a soft cry.

She began to run up the steps, up and up, till her breath burned in her chest. Once her feet slipped on the smooth, treacherous stone, and she nearly fell. She slowed and went more cautiously. Looking up, she could not see anyone, only the blank face of moon-bleached stone. These were not the steps she'd come up before. They led to a different and more sinister place. No sentries keeping watch. Nobody in the moonlight. Nobody in the shadows. She was on a wide and empty ledge, just over a man's height from the top of the outer wall and surrounded on its three other sides by lower walls, coming no higher than her waist. A lopsided stone box without a lid, and only two ways out: down the steps up which she'd come or through the dark square opening ahead of her.

She walked over to this opening, sat on the sill, and looked down into the ravine. Down and down, a sheer drop into the dark. No slope with bushes and weeds to cling to, no ledges or knobs freckling the smooth vertical rock with fingerholds, nothing but a rapid plunge into the dark. How many men had been thrust screaming through this cold door to shatter on the stones below?

"Phaidon! Phaidon!" she called, but the only answer was the echo of her own unhappy voice.

And yet she had heard a cry. She was sure she had heard a cry. She hung right out over the ravine, her fingers gripping the stone to stop herself from falling, but she could see nothing in the mottled, moon-frosted depths, only tiny glints of light that could be reflected from wet leaves or stones or a dead boy's eyes.

I must go down! I must get a rope! Nothing to tie it on to . . . Dorian can hold it and lower me. . . . Phaidon can't be dead! He can't! I heard a cry.

She began running down the steps again as fast as she dared and did not hear above the sound of her feet on the stone and her loud, ragged breathing, the owls crying to each other on the mountainside.

CHAPTER 24

The stout woman had won her argument with the sergeant of the guards quite easily, being helped by the reluctance of his own men to kill the boy.

"All right, take him, but it's your fault if anything goes wrong!" he said.

The woman shrugged. She took Phaidon through a door and down a long passage, lit by torches fixed to the walls. The shining floor reflected the flames like pools of liquid fire around their feet. The walls themselves were painted with strange designs: Eyes without faces looked out at him, birds spread their wings, and snakes stood upon their tails.

"In here go," the woman said, opening another door and thrusting him inside.

He found himself in a large room, lit by what seemed a hundred lamps. Everywhere light glittered in gold and silver: in plates and bowls and urns, in tiny figurines of strange gods and squinting cats.

In the center of the room was a splendid bed, carved out of ebony and inlaid with silver and mother-of-pearl. Instead of feet, it rested upon the backs of four ebony lions, with golden manes and silver teeth. At the head of the bed, half sitting and half lying on a tumble of furs and bright cushions, was what he first took for a sick child, so thin she was and sallow.

"I bring him, lady," the servant said, pushing Phaidon down on his knees so hard that he slid across the polished floor right up the queen's bed.

The queen giggled. Her laughter was taken up by the other women in the room, who were lounging on chairs and cushions near a table laden with bowls of fruit and nuts, plates of cheese and honey cakes and silver jugs.

While they laughed at him, Phaidon looked at everything from beneath his lashes and then back at the bed. So this was the queen, sitting like a spoiled child at a secret feast with her women. Laughing at him as she no doubt laughed at her ugly old husband, making a game of him behind his back. A dangerous game to play with a violent and powerful king, a game that could end in death. Melos had told him why the people were so anxious that the queen should recover. Not because they loved her, how could they? Even before she had become ill, she'd sulked in her rooms, hating everything about Anaktaron, only going out hunting with her brother, who had come with her, and crying for a week when he'd returned to Egypt. They prayed for her health only because their king had a habit of going to war when he was unhappy or angry, picking quarrels with his neighbors and trying to forget his grief in battle. They had lost too many of their young men that way. They prayed that the king would be happy in his marriage, have fine children, and stay at home.

The queen stopped laughing and looked at him with her eyebrows raised.

"So you are the birthday gift my royal husband send me?" she asked. Her accent was only slight, far less than her servant's. "You look a little worse for wear. Did he tell you to scream so loud under my window, eh, boy?"

"They were going to kill me!" Phaidon cried.

"Who? The guards? Why, what bad thing have you done?"

"Nothing, lady! I swear I haven't done anything! I was just standing there, but the king got into a rage, and—"

"And you were the dog he kicked, eh?"

"I tell you, lady," her maid said. "I tell you you go too far one day."

"Be quiet, Henet!" the queen ordered angrily. "Watch your tongue or I'll cut it out." She turned back to Phaidon and said, with the little smile of a pleased cat, "So the king was angry when he heard I wasn't coming?"

"Yes, lady. And all your people were silent and afraid."

"They're not my people," she said, frowning.

"I'm sorry. They called you their queen, so I thought—"

"Never mind what you thought. You know nothing. Sing me a song and get it over with. I don't find you amusing after all."

All Phaidon's songs deserted him. The bright, glittering room, heavy with scent and smoke from too many lamps, confused him. The strange young queen made him nervous. He felt sorry for the ugly, baffled king. A woman like this could drive people mad, darting and stinging like a mosquito. Phaidon could see nothing in her to love. She wasn't even pretty. Though she was thin, as thin as Iris, she did not look ill. Her skin was sallow, but a few days in the sun would put that right. Her hair, black and straight and heavy as a horse's tail, shone with life and health, and her full lips were red. Her eyes were large and black and heavily outlined with kohl, but he'd seen more beautiful women walking around the palace.

"Now I have offend him," the queen said, and her women laughed. "Here, boy, have a grape——" She broke one off the bunch she was holding in her hand and put it into his mouth. "There. Get off your knees and sing me a song. That is what you are for, isn't it?"

Phaidon stood up, and someone thrust a lyre into his hands. His face was stiff with bruises, and there was a small cut on the side of his mouth. His mind was empty, but his fingers played the plaintive melody that had been haunting him for days, and the words came back to him. He began to sing softly:

> *I never know if she can hear me*
> *Sadly singing in the night.*
> *Is she far away or near me?*
> *In some palace out of sight*
> *Is she waiting all alone?*
>
> *In this game of hunt-the-sister,*
> *Am I hot or am I cold?*
> *Will I find her, have I missed her,*
> *Must I seek till I am old*
> *For a maiden made of stone?*
>
> *Never will there come an answer,*
> *Lips of marble can't reply.*
> *Frozen is the pretty dancer.*
> *Eyes of marble cannot cry*
> *For a brother on his own.*

All his past fear and unhappiness had been in his voice. When he finished singing, there was a silence. Then the queen rubbed her eyes with her knuckles. "You make me cry and smudge my kohl. Why you sing so sad about brother and sister? And the words . . . is your sister dead?"

"Yes," Phaidon said, and could not go on.

He felt her thin arms around his shoulders. "Ah, poor boy! Come sit beside me. We must comfort each other. I know a little of that sorrow. I have lost a brother, though he is not dead. My family, my home, my country—I lost them all when I marry, and gained what? I am queen of this—" She broke off and made a gesture with her hands that seemed to dismiss the gorgeous room, her royal husband, and the whole of Anaktaron, as if they were nothing. "Come, tell me about your sister, and we'll be sad together."

So Phaidon sat on the royal bed, with the queen feeding him grapes as if he were a pet monkey, and told her about Cleo's being turned to stone and then stolen from them and how he'd vowed to the gods that he'd find her one day and give her a proper burial, with all the necessary rites.

The queen understood this completely, for she was an Egyptian and such things were important to her, too. "Of course. It is your duty as her brother, your father being dead. It is a pity that you have lost her, but never mind. I will tell the king he must help you and give you horses and gold when you set out to look for her. Why you look like that?"

"Lady, the king won't want to help me," Phaidon said unhappily. "He—he told the guards to get rid of me."

"Ah, yes, he is angry. It is natural he want them to throw you out. But kill you? No, that I do not believe. The guards are stupid and misunderstand. We will have them killed instead."

He could not tell if she was serious or not. "One of them is my friend. He asked his sergeant to let me go."

"Then we will kill the sergeant. No? You do not want that either? As you wish, we will kill nobody." She got up from her bed and stretched her arms, yawning. "So I go to the feast after all, because you remind me of my young brother. I hope you are grateful. It is so boring. The men talk about war, and the women—oh, I don't care what the women say. I don't listen to them. Now be off with you while I change my dress. I must make myself beautiful, for my maid Henet say the king is angry with me. She say one day I go too far and he kill me."

"Lady, I only try to warn you," the maid said anxiously.

Her mistress laughed and told her not to worry. "I do not cut out a faithful tongue. I am a princess of Egypt, not a savage," she said grandly. "Boy, take these cushions for my couch and tell the king I am coming. Henet will show you the way."

CHAPTER 25

Henet brought him out of the door at the head of the marble steps that led down to the great courtyard. Immediately they were challenged by a guard.

"What do you mean, 'Who goes there?' " she demanded irritably. "You know me. I am Henet, the queen's maid. You see me many times. I do not change my name since breakfast."

"Ah, I know you all right, pretty Henet," the guard said, laughing at her. "But who is this hiding behind a pile of cushions, eh?" He lifted the top cushion off, revealing Phaidon's dismayed face. "Ye gods, it's the boy singer. Are you mad, Henet? The king will eat him. Get him out of the way before he sees him."

"The queen give him message for the king," Henet said, shrugging. "He tell king message, he can go. Not my business."

Phaidon glanced down the steps into the crowded courtyard below. The king was sitting with his back to them. He could not see his face but guessed the thick black brows must be scowling from the nervous way the people near him behaved. They ate their food quickly and talked in low voices, drinking very little in case a wine-loosened tongue betrayed them into an unlucky remark and brought down the king's anger on their heads. There was very little noise. Melos was playing an old song about wine and friendship, but nobody was singing.

Smoke from the burning torches drifted up the steps, making Phaidon's eyes sting. He was afraid it would look as if he'd been crying.

"Can't you give the king the message, Henet?" the guard asked. "The king won't be angry with you. I'd do it myself, only I'm not allowed to leave this door."

But the maid shook her head, pretending not to understand, and retreated into the building.

"Sorry, lad, it'll have to be you," the guard said. "No knives on you, are there? Let me see those cushions. Right. Now hold your arms out from your sides while I check. . . . That's right. Nothing there. Here are your cushions back. I should keep your face hidden. Hold them up and away from your body, so that you can see where to put your feet. That's right. Good luck to you."

Phaidon went down the steps carefully, hoping he'd look like any slave fetching and carrying for his master. The low murmur of voices died away. The music stopped on a discord. All he could hear now was the sound of his sandals clapping the marble steps. He had a horrible feeling that everyone was staring at him and couldn't think why. Then, looking down for the next step, he noticed that his long legs were smudged with blood and dust, above the distinctive silver sandals on his feet. What was the good of hiding his face when his feet gave him away?

There were people sitting on the bottom steps. As he hesitated, wondering which way to go, he heard them whisper, "Hide, lad!

Crouch down behind us. Don't let the king see you. He's in a filthy temper. Hide!"

"I can't," he said regretfully. "I have a message from the queen."

He had spoken in a low voice, but the king, hearing the word *queen*, thrust back his chair and turned to see what everyone was staring at.

"What was that? What did you say about the queen? Come here!"

Phaidon pushed his way through the people and went down on his knees, scattering the cushions around him.

"Great lord, the queen is coming!" he cried.

The king got slowly to his feet and glared down at him. He did not say anything.

"She thanks you for the gift you sent her," Phaidon went on quickly.

"Gift? What gift?"

"I think she meant me," Phaidon said, embarrassed. "She said you wanted me to sing for her birthday, so I did, my lord. And then, it was like magic, her illness was gone." (This was what the queen had instructed him to say. "Tell him your song cured me like magic," she'd said, laughing.)

Immediately whispers rustled through the crowd like the wind through dead leaves. He heard the word *oracle* repeated and saw they were staring at him with awe. Suddenly he felt frightened and wished he had not used the word *magic*.

The king, however, did not seem impressed.

"It's the first time I've heard of a song curing a headache," he said. "Music certainly doesn't have that effect on me. How do you explain it, boy? And aren't you the boy I asked the guards to turn out of the gates? How is it you're still here, though somewhat bruised and battered since I last saw you? Don't tell me you got away from them, three large soldiers like that?"

So the queen was right: The king had not meant him to be killed. He might have been more careful choosing his words. . . .

"The queen heard me shouting and sent her maid to fetch me, my lord."

"And then you sang to her and cured her by magic? Are you claiming to be the bird of the oracle, is that it?"

Phaidon hesitated. Then something impelled him to say honestly, "No, my lord. I'm not a healer. I can't do magic. I'm just a boy, a singer. But ever since I've been here, people have talked about the oracle as if—as if I were somehow part of it. I don't see I can be. We came here by accident. We were lost in a fog at sea, and then the sky cleared and the wind blew us to your shores. I'd never even heard of Anaktaron until—"

"Until what?" the king asked quietly.

"Until the lady Atropos mentioned it."

"*Atropos?* What did she say?"

"She and her sisters were waiting on the road above the bay, looking out to sea. When she saw me, she said, 'See you in Anaktaron,' and they all rode away."

"And what did you make of that?"

"I thought she'd mistaken me for someone else, my lord."

The king laughed and waved him away, saying mildly, "Go and sit down by Melos. When the queen comes, you can entertain us with your songs. Leave the cushions." As Phaidon turned away, he heard him say to Lord Telamon, "The innocent bird who denies death? You're right. It's an odd coincidence. It makes one wonder. . . ."

Phaidon joined Melos and sat at his feet. The old minstrel smiled down at him. Seeing Phaidon's eyes searching the crowd, he whispered, "Your family followed you when the guards carried you off. I expect they're still searching for you. Don't worry. They'll be all right. You must stay here now, Phaidon. You'll be needed when the queen comes. Pray that she doesn't change her mind."

She did not keep them waiting long. Perhaps she had meant to come all the time. Perhaps she thought she had tried the patience of the king a little too far. She appeared at the top of the stairs, supported by her ladies, a gauzy figure in a green dress, thin as a blade of grass, and wearing an elaborate collar of gold and copper and colored stones that looked heavy enough to weigh down a cart horse. It showed off the delicate bones of her face and the graceful curve of her long neck. For the first time Phaidon saw that she was beautiful, in her odd way.

The king ran up the steps to meet her, caught her up in his arms, and carried her down to her cushioned couch.

"She's got away with it again," Melos whispered. "Let's hope she's learned her lesson this time. Come, lad, it's time for your songs."

So Phaidon sang his songs of love and war. He sang his monster song, and the soldiers joined in the chorus, stamping their feet on the floor. The queen laughed her clear, childish laugh and clapped her hands. Then the king took a ring from his finger and threw it to Phaidon, who caught it neatly and bowed his thanks.

"Never part with it," Melos whispered. "It's a mark of high honor, a ring from the king's own hand. I'll say this for him. He may be a bad-tempered old bear, but he never forgets a favor. You and your family have a home here for as long as you wish."

Phaidon was dazed with happiness. Everywhere he looked, he saw faces smiling at him. His uncle, Dorian, and Gordius were back, and even as he looked, he saw Iris slip through the pillars, stare when she saw him, and then smile with joy. She'd been crying, a tear still hung on her wet cheek like a gold bead in the torchlight, but soon, as she started jumping up and down and waving, it dropped and was gone.

His bruises ached, and the cut on his lips stung when he sang, but he didn't care. He was alive. The people loved him again and cheered every song. He was their oracle boy who had denied death and saved their queen. It was no good his saying he was an ordinary boy; they didn't believe him.

"He fought us like a young lion," the guard Nikos told everyone who would listen. "See how he's bruised all over and his lip bleeds, yet still he sings like a bird. He refused to go to his death. He said he had better things to do."

"I didn't, I'm sure I didn't," Phaidon protested later. "You mustn't believe what they say, or I won't know who I am. They so want me to be their oracle boy, they're changing everything. They're making me up as they go along."

He was walking back to the guesthouse with Iris and Gordius. His uncle and Dorian had gone ahead. The birthday celebrations were over. The king and queen had retired, and only a few drunken revelers were left, huddled around the fire in the great courtyard. At dawn an army of slaves would come and sweep and scrub and polish, but at the moment it was quiet and cool. Phaidon half wished he could stay here with his friends forever. *Seven days*, he thought, *I'll give myself seven days, and then I must be gone. I won't tell the others in case they think they ought to offer to come with me. They'll be safe here. I made the vow to the gods. It's my responsibility. I can't let poor Cleo down. . . . I wish I were braver. How will I manage all by myself?*

"Your uncle said he had some food for us," Iris said, interrupting his thoughts. "I'm hungry, aren't you? I missed all the feast, looking for you. I thought you were dead. I wept so many tears into the ravine that I nearly turned Anaktaron into an island. I wish it was an island. I miss the sea, don't you? When are we going to start on our travels, Phaidon?"

"*You're* not going anywhere," he said, staring. "You're staying here with the others. Melos said the king will let us stay here as long as we wish."

"That's good," she said cheerfully. "That takes care of your uncle. And Dorian, too. I think he should stay here and learn his new craft. It'd be a pity to miss the chance. But Gordius and I are coming with you. It's all decided, so don't waste your breath arguing."

Atropos and her two old sisters rode out of Anaktaron the day after the feast. Dressed all in black, they sat on their mules like three crows, and people watched them uneasily as they went by, glad they were going but not wanting to show it, for the sisters were said to have supernatural powers.

Only Phaidon, hanging around the gates, greeted them with a smile, bearing them no grudge for the bath they'd given him when he'd first arrived.

"Are you going so soon?" he asked. "I won't be long behind you. I meant to set out in a few days, but everyone says I must stay longer. They say the king will take it as an insult if I leave too soon. I don't know what to do."

Atropos reined in her mule. "You will stay here nearly three years," she told him, "then you and your young wife and your friend Gordius—"

"My wife?" he said, laughing up at her. "I'm not married!"

"You will marry the girl Iris," she said. "Then, when the war is over—"

"What war?"

"The war that prevents you, among other things, from leaving Anaktaron sooner. The dead can wait, Phaidon. You must look after the living first. Then, at last, you and she and Gordius will set out to look for your sister."

"Will I find her?" he asked, fearing her answer.

"Yes and no," Atropos said, and rode away.

CHAPTER 26

Five years later, on a fine afternoon, with the sea showing so dark a blue between the bleached fields that it looked as if it had been painted, Phaidon, Iris, and Gordius rode down toward Telos. They rode slowly, for they had come a long way and had no reason to believe that this small palace would prove to be the right one.

They had seen so many palaces. Traveled so far, over mountains and plains, through forests and across rivers, singing for their supper wherever they found people to listen. When they found nobody to give them food and shelter for the night, they lived off the land as best they could, sleeping in dry caves or under dripping bushes.

Sometimes they met up with other travelers and rode with them, glad of their company, for a large party was in less danger from the robbers who haunted the woods and lonely paths, and they were carrying hidden gold. Their new companions, noticing their lyres, would offer them food and wine in exchange for their songs and stories.

They had many adventures to tell now. There was the great siege of Anaktaron and how the king had outwitted his enemies, obtaining supplies through an underground passage that led to one of his own hill farms. There was the bear Iris claimed must have been her foster brother, who had shared their cave one night, unknown to them while they slept. When Iris, waking, had squealed to see it, it had sniffed at her, smiled, and shambled away.

"Don't tell people it smiled," Phaidon advised her. "They won't swallow that."

"But it did. I saw it," she said.

"Bears always look as if they are smiling," Gordius told them. "A hunter told me that once. He said that's what makes them so dangerous. You think they're friendly, and then they eat you."

Then there was the talking tree, which claimed it had once been a woman, the wolf that had sat down before them and howled most piteously and drawn pictures in the dust with its paw, and many other strange and sometimes dangerous adventures. All these Phaidon made songs about. His voice, though it had broken long before they left Anaktaron, was as beautiful as ever and had a great range, so that he could sing both high and low. Melos had trained him well.

Iris never learned to sing quite in tune, but she told her stories so vividly, in her off-key but oddly attractive voice, that she was in great demand. And Gordius, while they entertained their hosts, repaired everything with his clever hands, from bridles to earthenware pots, bronze urns, weapons, knives, and even the most delicate jewelry.

So they had traveled, sometimes wet and cold, but more often as happy as princes, eating the best food, sleeping in soft beds, and riding merrily in the sun. The wandering life suited them. When they were older, they said, it would be time enough to settle down.

"When we have children, Phaidon," Iris said, "we'll need a cart to carry them in, until they're old enough to ride. And you will teach them to sing."

Phaidon laughed and hugged her, reminding her that they had promised to return one day to Anaktaron, where the king had said there'd always be a home for them, and they would see his uncle and Dorian again.

So, talking, they rode down to Telos in the afternoon sunlight, hoping for no more than a friendly welcome, a good meal, and, with luck, an invitation to stay for a while. They did not know that in this small and rather shabby palace, with plants growing from cracks in its outer walls, they would find at last what they were looking for.

She was in a quiet courtyard, overlooking the sea: the stone figure of a girl, holding in her hands a silver jug.

How small she is, he thought, *how young. Is this my older sister, this child, gazing out at the world with laughing astonishment, as if her stone eyes see some marvel invisible to me?*

It was Cleo, yet it was not. Yes and no, as Atropos had said. Cleo's spirit was not trapped in the stone but was as free as air. She had no need for his tears. Yet kneeling before the stone figure, half child, half woman, he wept for his dead sister, who would never grow any older.

Iris, watching him, wept, too, for his sorrow and for the girl she had never known. But when at last he got to his feet and turned to her, she saw he was smiling.

"Don't cry for her," he said gently, wiping a tear from her cheek with his thumb. "There's no need. She's happy here, can't you feel it? This is a beautiful place. Look at the sea, how bright it is. She always loved the sea." He looked around the courtyard. There were pots of flowers by the wall. Some child had left its doll on the warm paving stone. The air was fresh with the tang of the sea. "It seems a pity to shut her away in the dark," he said.

She stared at him, worried. "But, Phaidon, you promised the gods you'd give her a proper tomb. And the prince here has been so kind, saying he'd do everything he could to help you build a tomb for her here. He even offered to arrange for a ship to take her back to the coast below Anaktaron, if that was what you wanted. Which was very generous of him, Phaidon, as he can't have known you have any gold. Unless you told him?"

Phaidon did not answer. His eyes were fixed on the sea and dreaming.

"I'll build her the most beautiful tomb in the world, near here where she can see the sea," he said. "I'll do everything I vowed to do, and then we'll be happy, won't we, Iris? We won't have to look back."

Just outside the palace at Telos there is now a small but very beautiful building overlooking the sea. People seeing it for the first time take it for a temple, for the roof is supported by painted pillars, and it is open to the air except for a curved wall at the back. They are surprised when they are told that it is the tomb of Cleo, the young sister of the famous singer Phaidon of Anaktaron.

Inside the building the statue of a pretty young girl smiles out at the bright world. In her hands she holds a silver jug, which the local children fill with flowers. Women in love with sailors come to beg her to ask Poseidon for favorable winds, for it is said that her brother dedicated her tomb to the sea god, with all the proper rites. Some people, sitting around their fires at night whisper that the statue is not really a statue at all but is the dead girl herself, who was turned to stone by the Gorgon's head.

Phaidon and his young wife come to visit her often, and if you're lucky, you can hear him singing to the sea god:

May your sea nymphs sing and play
Softly while my sister sleeps.
May your winds blow harm away
From the sanctuary she keeps.
From all calamity that shakes
The hearts of men, let her escape.
The fire that burns, the blood that makes
The sea as purple as the grape,
The fighting ship, the ravaged field—
Keep them away from her. And long
Shall we our thanks and praises yield
To great Poseidon in our song.